"Feel free to detour in my direction anytime,"

he said. "It can get lonesome here."

Shawna wondered if he really was lonely in his isolated cottage. If he was, she knew it was by choice. A man like Kurt Slater could have his pick of friends—and female companions. He was definitely a charmer.

But Shawna wouldn't let him charm her. He was the enemy, the man who'd wrought pain and suffering into the lives of people she loved.

No, she would never fall under the hypnotic spell of those sea-green eyes. *Just you wait, Kurt Slater*, she vowed. *By hook or by crook, I'm going to uncover the truth!*

Dear Reader:

The spirit of the Silhouette Romance Homecoming Celebration lives on as each month we bring you six books by continuing stars!

And we have a galaxy of stars planned for 1988. In the coming months, we're publishing romances by many of your favorite authors such as Annette Broadrick, Sondra Stanford and Brittany Young. And that's not all—during the summer, Diana Palmer presents her most engaging heroes and heroines in a trilogy that will be sure to capture your heart!

Your response to these authors and other authors of Silhouette Romances has served as a touchstone for us, and we're pleased to bring you more books with Silhouette's distinctive medley of charm, wit and—above all—romance.

I hope you enjoy this book and the many stories to come. Come home to romance—for always!

Sincerely,

Tara Hughes
Senior Editor
Silhouette Books

JOAN SMITH

By Hook or By Crook

Silhouette *Romance*

Published by Silhouette Books New York

America's Publisher of Contemporary Romance

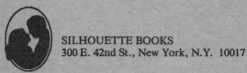 SILHOUETTE BOOKS
300 E. 42nd St., New York, N.Y. 10017

ISBN: 0-373-08591-5

First Silhouette Books printing July 1988

Printed in the U.S.A.

Books by Joan Smith

Silhouette Romance

Next Year's Blonde #234
Caprice #255
From Now On #269
Chance of a Lifetime #288
Best of Enemies #302
Trouble in Paradise #315
Future Perfect #325
Tender Takeover #343
The Yielding Art #354
The Infamous Madam X #430
Where's There's a Will #452
Dear Corrie #546
If You Love Me #562
By Hook or By Crook #591

JOAN SMITH

has written many Regency romances but likes working with the greater freedom of contemporaries. She also enjoys mysteries and Gothics, collects Japanese porcelain and is a passionate gardener. A native of Canada, she is the mother of three.

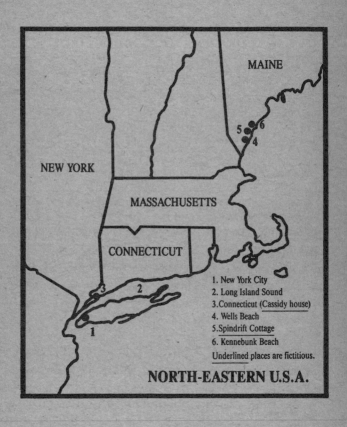

1. New York City
2. Long Island Sound
3. Connecticut (Cassidy house)
4. Wells Beach
5. Spindrift Cottage
6. Kennebunk Beach

Underlined places are fictitious.

NORTH-EASTERN U.S.A.

Chapter One

The moon was hidden beyond mist-laden clouds, casting a luminous, opal haze across the sky. Moonlight shimmered on the water below, a silvery sheen, dancing along the rippled surface. Out on the point, a lighthouse rose like a giant flashlight switching on and off with hypnotic regularity. A light breeze cooled the sultry July air, carrying the tang of salt and seaweed, that unmistakable smell of the sea. It was a perfect night.

Shawna Cassidy, oblivious to her surroundings, peered into the shadows and muttered, "Dammit! Doesn't he *ever* leave his cottage?"

The lights had been burning in Kurt Slater's gray Cape Cod cottage ever since dusk. How could she get inside and search if he never left? So far, she'd only seen him from a distance. Of course, that was enough to recognize the great Slater. At first glance, anyone would take him for an actor, and not the bright new star of the fashion-designing firmament, a title that Shawna grudgingly conceded to. For Slater's path to fame had been paved with treachery.

The coveted Golden Needle Award for excellence in design—the honor that should have gone to her Uncle Max for his fall and winter collection—had been given to Slater. Shawna intended to get into that cottage, by hook or by crook, and see if Slater had stolen Maxwell Everett's ideas for his new spring line as well. If Slater ever left his cottage, that is. She'd been watching and waiting since four in the afternoon, and so far he hadn't gone beyond view of his own front door.

A glance at her watch told her it was ten o'clock. Shawna had been up since seven that morning, driven from New York to the south coast of Maine, gone grocery shopping, and installed herself in the rented cottage. Now she wanted nothing more than to fall into bed. Exasperation gnawed at her. In a fit of frustration, she said, "To hell with it. I'm going to peek in his window and see what he's doing."

She kicked off her sandals and ran down to the beach. The wet sand felt soft and surprisingly cool, like walking on sherbet. A mist of spray blew off the sea's surface and cooled her bare legs. Spindrift, that spray was called. Slater's cottage was about two hundred yards north along the coast. Running now, Shawna left the beach and angled her way to the lighted window. The only sound was the gentle hissing of the tide, and the beating of her heart.

By standing on tiptoe, she could just see into Slater's living room. It was large, square, whitewashed and timbered. She was surprised to see the furnishings were comfortable rather than grand. The wall was decorated with the traditional miscellany of lobster traps and nets, spangled with the pretty colored-glass balls that were used for trap markers. A good seascape done in oils hung over the fieldstone fireplace. Shawna hardly glanced at the decor, her eyes were soon riveted on Kurt Slater.

Or to be more precise, on Kurt Slater's back. He sat on a high stool, hunched over a drawing board, and from where Shawna stood, he looked stark naked. His broad, tanned back was unflawed by so much as one tiny mole or freckle. Muscles rippled smoothly as he moved his arm. A silken cap of chestnut hair gleamed amid the light of a lamp. The back of his hair was long, hugging his neck. With a reluctant admiration for his physique, Shawna moved closer, trying to see what he was sketching.

She drew in her breath sharply. He was drawing a woman, but what surprised her was that the tall, rangy redhead could have been her. The hair in particular caused her to gasp in surprise. Not many women had copper-bright hair. To soften the effect, Shawna let the top grow longer and wore it brushed aside in a natural wave. Of course it spent half its time falling in her eyes—just like the woman in the sketch.

He'd been spying on *her*! Pretending he didn't even see her when he went jogging along the beach with his ugly old dog. He must have eyes in the back of his head, she mused. He had certainly drawn her shape right—or her lack of shape. Suddenly the inadequacies of her body were all too obvious, since the model in his sketch wasn't wearing any clothes yet.

She found it disconcerting that Slater sat staring at that naked body, his hand poised just at her breast. He cocked his head aside and went on gazing. After a moment, his hand moved swiftly and his model appeared gowned in black lines, which were soon shaded in sea-foam green. A straight band covered her breasts and nipped into a small waist. Below, a billow of sea foam made her look as though she were Venus, rising from the waves. Nice. *Very* nice, and so effortless! If he could create his own designs so effortlessly, why did he bother pirating Everett's?

As Shawna pondered this puzzle, Slater rose and left the room. She noticed that his jeans, cutoff shorts, rode dangerously low on his hips. His long legs were well muscled, straight and as brown as his back. On his feet he wore moccasins without any socks. Despite these casual rags, he looked as elegant as a duke. It was the proud way he walked, with his head high and his shoulders swaggering that lent him that air of distinction. A moment later, Slater reappeared carrying an open can of beer. As he stood examining his sketch, Shawna scrutinized his face.

He reminded her of a savage. His weathered cheekbones were high and prominent, sheering away to lean cheeks, and ending in a jaw that was geometrically squared. His dark, high-arched eyebrows made him look intrigued or questioning. The shock of hair that tumbled over his forehead was sun bleached to toffee in front. If Shawna had been an artist, she would have completed his severe face with thin lips. His full, sensuously carved lips lifted in a smile as he examined his sketch. They lent an air of interesting incongruity to his appearance.

With one hand, he reached up and ran his fingers lightly over the patch of hair on his chest. Shawna felt a shiver, light as a pair of tiny mice feet, pattering up her spine. He held the can to his lips, tilted his head back and drank. Kurt Slater even looked distinguished drinking beer from a can.

Slater's head turned sharply and Shawna ducked below the window. When she peeped in again, he was looking at his dog, who was just waddling out from a corner. Kurt smiled and said something to the dog. It was a black-and-white Border collie, wearing a mutinous expression. The dog went to the door, and as Kurt followed, it occurred to Shawna that he might be planning to let the dog out. She'd better get away—fast!

She left the window and flew into the shadows. Before she'd gone far, she heard the unmistakable yapping of the dog behind her. She ran faster, faster, till she was gasping for breath. The sand was soft and damp, clinging to her feet. She seemed to slow with every step, sinking into the velvety beach.

And that wasn't the worst of it. Before long, she heard a man's shout. Slater was after her now, too. She'd given the whole show away before she proved a thing. In her state of panic, the only word she could distinguish was "Stop!" shouted in a peremptory voice. Fat chance!

The dog certainly moved quickly for a creature with such short legs. Before Shawna got home, it was nipping at her heels, and Slater wasn't far behind. She realized she shouldn't go into her cottage—she should run somewhere else so Slater wouldn't know how to find her. But her lungs ached from running, and her breaths came in ragged gasps. Where else could she go but to her own cottage? This stretch of beach was isolated.

The dog was jumping at her legs now. When she tried to push it off with her foot, she lost her balance and went rolling in the sand. The black-and-white dog growled at her, knowing it had her cornered. All she saw was a pair of jaws, attached to floppy ears and determined eyes. The dog's panting gasps were as loud as her own. She sat, wondering if she dare move, or if that would make the dog latch onto her with those sharp teeth.

Five minutes earlier Shawna would have thought the worst thing that could happen was that Slater caught her. Actually it was a relief when he came and called off his dog.

"Down, Brix," he ordered. The unruly dog backed off, heeled and looked to its owner for approval. "Good girl." Slater leaned over and offered Shawna his hand. "Are you all right?" he asked.

She noted the tone of genuine concern in his deep voice. She couldn't help noticing the rest of him, too. Moonlight softened the savage lines of his face, glinting in his dark eyes, glowing on his broad, naked shoulders.

As he drew her to her feet, she realized he couldn't know she'd been peeking in his window. Perhaps he thought she'd just gone out for a walk along the beach. A wave of relief washed over her, and she quickly reviewed her strategy. It was time to turn the tables.

Wrenching free of his grip, she put her hands on her hips and glared at him. "I'm fine. No thanks to you and your mutt."

His hands went out in a gesture of apology. "She wouldn't have hurt you. Border collies are trained to round up—er, sheep. She's just trying to be friendly."

"I am not a sheep! And she has an odd idea of friendliness. She nearly killed me!"

His dark eyebrow rose higher and a light laugh hung on the air. This wasn't the way he'd have chosen to meet the enchanting redhead, but he'd just have to make the best of it. He wanted to reach out and push that sultry lock of hair out of her eyes, so he could see them more clearly. In the moonlight, it was impossible to tell what color her eyes were. Green was his bet, and he guessed that there was a smattering of freckles on the bridge of her nose, too. By the moon's silvery light he could see she was as pretty as he'd thought. Her stormy eyes were fringed with long lashes, and her upturned little nose looked saucy. Her full lower lip gave her the appearance of a sulky child.

"That's a slight exaggeration," he pointed out reasonably.

Shawna sniffed and began brushing the sand from her shorts. "There's a law against letting dogs run free, you know."

His eyes skimmed over her close-fitting cotton shirt, down to her shapely legs. She had a classic model's figure, long and willowy. Models often rented the Carters' cottage. Kurt had always assumed his own presence next door had something to do with it. But when models came chasing after him to Maine, they certainly didn't just sit on their porches and ignore him. It was this redhead's standoffish behavior that first intrigued him. Brix emitted a bark, and Slater turned to pat her head.

"She says she's sorry," he interpreted. "I'm sorry, too. My name's Kurt. We're neighbors." He reached out his hand, and she accepted it. He had an honest handshake, firm without crippling her smaller hand, that seemed to disappear in his.

"Shawna Cassidy," she said.

"Can we walk you home?" He noticed that she didn't seem to recognize his name. Maybe he'd gotten lucky, and this woman didn't know who he was. On the other hand, he was more commonly known as Slater. He wouldn't tell her his last name, though—not yet.

Shawna swiftly assessed his offer. Since he'd said he was a neighbor, he obviously knew she was renting the Carters' cottage. It was only about ten yards away. "If you just hold on to Jaws, I think I can make it from here," she replied.

"Why don't we go in and check you out for damages?" he suggested. She gave him a doubtful look. "Seriously, I'd like to know you're all right."

Although Shawna's intention was to get into *his* cottage, letting him into hers seemed like a good first step. She'd have preferred searching his place when he was away, but since he stuck like glue, that might not be easy. And there was nothing in this cottage to let him know who she was. She'd tell him she was a secretary on vacation. Her name wouldn't mean anything to him, as she'd only joined Max Everett's firm a few months ago.

"All right," she said, with a hunch of her shoulders.

They walked along, sinking into the sand. "Are you staying long, Shawna?" he asked.

"Just a week. I'm here on vacation. How about you?"

"I live here, in the gray cottage next door."

She knew he "lived" in New York, but could hardly question his statement since she wasn't supposed to know anything about him.

"Are you alone?" he asked.

Suddenly her carefully contrived visit seemed suspect. Nobody spent their vacation all alone in an isolated cottage. Spindrift Cottage wasn't even in a town. It was halfway between Wells Beach and Kennebunk Beach.

"My girlfriend was supposed to come with me, but she couldn't get away. I came anyway, since we'd already paid for the cottage," she invented.

"Where are you from?"

"Lewiston."

"You didn't have far to come."

"I've always loved the ocean," she said. That, at least, was true. She'd grown up in a place something like this, on Long Island Sound, at the southwestern tip of Connecticut. It had been handy to her mother's modeling work in New York City in the early days, but without the hassle of city living.

Kurt stopped walking and stood gazing out at the ocean. "It's beautiful, isn't it?" His voice had a peaceful, faraway sound. When she peered up at him, his face mirrored the same feeling. It was an oddly placid expression for that savage face. The unusual combination intrigued her.

"Where are you from, Kurt?" she asked, and was disturbed to find herself beginning to take an interest in this man. He wasn't supposed to become a real person to her. He was the enemy, the man she had come here to outwit.

"From here," he said. "I was born in that cottage." He nodded down the beach toward his place.

"Oh, do your parents live there, too?" That would really complicate getting in!

"No, when Dad retired they moved to Arizona—for his rheumatism," he explained.

Brix decided to explore the beach, and they wandered down after her. Still barefoot, Shawna walked in the lapping foam. "It's cold," she said.

"You should feel it in winter."

"It must be freezing here, with the Atlantic gales!"

"It gets chilly," he said, lifting his brows to tell her it was an understatement. "But then when you pile driftwood in the fireplace and listen to the waves pounding outside, it's cozy."

Shawna pictured that old fieldstone fireplace, blazing in January, with the wind howling at the windows, and felt a wave of homesickness.

"But in any season, it's beautiful," Kurt continued. "I can't breathe away from the ocean. The old atavistic instinct, I guess. You must like it, too, since you came here alone?" He studied her, interested in her answer.

"Yes, I love it."

"We've found something in common already," he said, and smiled. A young woman from upstate obviously wasn't a model. She was just a working woman on vacation. "What are your feelings about lobster?"

"Broiled in the shell with clarified butter, I'd say they're right up there with ambrosia."

"I can get them fresh. I know the local fishermen. There's some interesting sight-seeing hereabouts, too. I'll take you on a tour, if you like."

Shawna was surprised at his friendliness, after he'd ignored her all day. In spite of her reason for being here, she was also a little flattered. "Are you vacationing, too?" she asked innocently.

"Not exactly. I work at home, on my own time."

"What do you do?" The question came out so naturally, it would almost have seemed odd not to have asked it.

There was a brief cut noticeable pause before he answered. "I'm sort of a commercial artist," Kurt replied, still leery of revealing his identity.

It wasn't exactly a lie, he rationalized to himself. But why had he said it? Was it because so many women threw themselves at Kurt Slater? He wouldn't mind if Shawna wanted to hurl herself in his direction, but it would be nice to know it was him the women liked, and not his reputation.

"What sort?" she asked.

"A pretty good one, I think," he replied evasively, and laughed. Before she could follow it up, he said, "How about you?"

"I'm a secretary in a real estate office."

He would have thought she'd be a teacher or a nurse. "Is that how you heard Carters' cottage was for rent?"

"No, actually I answered an ad in the paper." Shawna told as much of the truth as she could. She had carefully combed the ads, looking for a place close to Kurt Slater's, and had had the incredible good fortune to find the cottage right next door.

They turned to her cottage as they talked, and began walking toward it. It was a simple, white clapboard, three-bedroom cottage with a red shingle roof.

"Spindrift Cottage," Kurt said, gazing at it pensively. "I thought Mrs. Carter would sell it when her husband died, but instead she took an apartment in Kennebunk and rents the cottage during the summer. I guess she wants Joe to have it—that's her son. He works in California. But he'll probably end up selling it when he finally does inherit it."

"You can't live other people's lives for them. She might as well sell."

"I can understand her feelings. I'd like my son to go on living here after I'm gone. Or at least to come here for vacations. Roots, you know . . ." He looked once more out at the rolling ocean.

Shawna knew Kurt was unmarried, and didn't have to ask if this son was a reality or only a dream. But this wasn't the kind of talk she expected to hear from Kurt Slater. He was supposed to be a jaded businessman, more interested in fame, fortune and philandering than family roots. If she wasn't careful, she'd start liking him. But he's a thief, she reminded herself sternly. And you are not going to invite a thief into your cottage to "examine you for damages."

Brix decided she was missing something and ran, tongue lolling, to join them. "You mind your manners in the lady's house, Brix," Kurt ordered.

It was time to disillusion him about entering the cottage. "Thanks for the escort," she said, "but you don't have to come in. I'm fine."

Kurt looked at her questioningly. He didn't want to be pushy, but he didn't want to leave yet, either.

"I'm just going to take a shower and go to bed," she continued. "I've been up since seven this morning. After the trip, I'm bushed."

His eyebrows lifted in surprise. "You're not much of a traveler! It's only seventy miles from upstate."

Shawna swallowed a gasp of surprise. How had she made that mistake? "I didn't come directly. I detoured to visit some friends."

He hunched his strong shoulders. Suddenly he didn't look savage at all—merely disappointed.

"Feel free to detour in my direction any time. It can get lonesome here," he said.

Shawna wondered if he really was lonesome, alone in his cottage. He'd been there all day, without company. But it must be by choice. Kurt Slater could have his pick of friends. He was a handsome, successful businessman, in an industry swarming with beautiful women. And according to the gossip columns, he was no hermit. Shawna kept a close guard on her tongue this time. "You're a local boy. You must know people around here."

"I do, but I've been working pretty hard."

"Maybe you'll show me some of your work tomorrow," she suggested.

"Maybe, if you're interested. Well, if you're sure you're all right, Shawna, I'll take Brix home now. I'm glad we had this chance to meet—even if the circumstances weren't ideal.'' He reached out and patted her hand. His gentle touch surprised her.

Then he turned and called Brix. Kurt and the ungainly dog ran off together along the beach, and Shawna went into Spindrift Cottage. She was unhappy with the meeting. Kurt Slater wasn't at all what she'd expected. The man who was pirating Uncle Max's designs and claiming them for his own should be a sinister man, nasty and unattractive.

And Slater was certainly stealing Everett's designs. In the fall and winter show that was held in late March, the resemblance in work between the two designers was perfectly obvious to Shawna. And it was that collection that had won Kurt the Golden Needle Award. He had changed Everett's designs, made them more daring, used different materials and colors, but the basic line was just plain stolen.

Everett had even figured out how the theft was accomplished. His trusted personal assistant, Nancy Alton, had been going out with Kurt at the time. Naturally, she hadn't told Everett, but she'd been spotted, and word got back. Although Nancy had worked for him for ten years, Everett was forced to fire her. It was a terrible betrayal. And yet, Everett was too overwrought to take action against her; he didn't want to disgrace Nancy publicly.

But next year's spring and summer lines were being prepared now, and someone had broken into Everett's office and stolen a group of sketches. Everett seemed more depressed than angry. He was getting on in years, of course. He tried to maintain his youthful image, but Shawna knew he was in his sixties.

Although Everett was really no relation to Shawna, she'd called him Uncle Max all her life. Her mother had been his top model when she was young and Maxwell Everett was at his peak. He was a frequent guest at their house in Connecticut, and when her mother brought Shawna in to New York, it was always Uncle Max who entertained them. There were lavish restaurants and shows, carriage rides in Central Park and visits to galleries. He was like a doting surrogate uncle, and she would not let Kurt Slater or anyone else break his spirit.

"I hardly enjoy the work any longer," he had admitted with a weary sigh after the last break-in. "It wasn't always this way. It used to be fun; now it's just a business. I don't need the money. Why bother working so hard, only to have some young pirate come along and steal my work?"

"I think you should call the police, Everett," Shawna had told him. She had stopped calling him Uncle Max when she went to work for him a year ago. Everyone at the shop called him Everett, and she wanted to be treated like any other employee.

"Slater won't have kept the sketches. He'll just memorize them and adapt them, lowering a neckline here, adding a pleat there, destroying the integrity of the design. And for that he won the Golden Needle! Even the judges today don't appreciate good work. Things were different in the old days."

"Maybe he *did* keep the sketches. At least the unfavorable publicity will alert the industry that Slater's up to no good!"

"Without proof, it only looks like jealousy on my part to involve the prizewinner in a scandal. And even if he was so unwise as to keep the sketches, they wouldn't be in his New York office. He has a place in Maine that he slips away to, to do his altering—which he calls designing." Everett gave a sniff of disdain.

That was when Shawna got her idea. She had two weeks' vacation coming up. She'd go down to this place in Maine and, somehow, snoop around Slater's cottage and find evidence of what he was doing. At the very least, she'd discovered what he was designing for the next season's line, and if it bore a strong resemblance to Everett's stolen works, she would confront Kurt Slater herself. She'd threaten to announce what he was doing. Such a threat wouldn't give her the full satisfaction of seeing him behind bars, but at least it would bring his thievery to an end.

Everett had forbidden her scheme at first, but she'd eventually persuaded him to let her give it a shot. In the end, he'd revised her plan a little. "Don't take any sketches you find," he told her, "or you could be arrested."

"But if he has the stolen sketches, I'll call in the police," she said.

"If you find irrevocable proof, call me. But I'm afraid that all you'll find is his new designs. The thing to do is take a camera and photograph them. If they resemble mine closely, I'll speak to him. That would be better than calling the local police. I'm sure that Slater is on good terms with them. They wouldn't listen to you. I should really go with you myself, but Slater would recognize me in a minute."

"I'll only be gone a week. And I'll keep in touch, Everett."

"Will you tell Adele what you're doing?" Everett asked. Adele was her mother, his ex-model and good friend.

"Yes. She's expecting me home for my vacation. Since I'll be missing the first week, I'll have to tell her."

"I'll run up to Connecticut to keep her from being lonesome."

Everett had always kept in touch with his favorite model. Since Adele's husband had died a few years ago, he'd begun to see more of her. Shawna's mother had always visited New York to see her daughter. Nowadays, each visit was also an opportunity to get together with her former employer. Shawna thought they might marry eventually, though neither of them had mentioned it. She thought Everett had always been a little in love with the beautiful Adele.

Shawna locked the cottage door, turned out the lights and went upstairs for a bath. The unhappy face in the bathroom mirror didn't bear much resemblance to Adele. Her mother was an elegant, raven-haired woman who exuded sophistication. Every feature was perfect, from her heart-shaped face and classically straight nose, down her long neck to her reed-thin body.

Shawna had inherited her father's coloring. Why couldn't she have inherited her mother's raven hair and flawless cream complexion? But no, she was stuck with red hair and freckles. Since she had her mother's willowy body, everyone urged her to take up modeling, but she'd never been interested in that.

Fashion was her life, and she wanted to be at the very core of it, designing the clothes—not just wearing them. One day the name Shawna Cassidy would be as famous as Everett, or Slater. Should she call her own line Cassidy, or Shawna? She smiled at herself in the mirror. That was a decision she wouldn't have to make for a few years. First she would apprentice with Everett till she knew the business inside and out, then she planned to strike out on her own.

Sport clothes were her main interest—and her forte. Everett was planning to expand into that line, but so far he didn't think her work was good enough to warrant production. She wasn't entirely satisfied with his reaction to her designs. Everett was more interested in appearance than function, but for sport clothes, wearability was important.

Shawna was a casual person; fancy gowns weren't her preference. She wanted to design shirts and shorts, skirts and slacks and jackets to be mixed and matched. She could still learn plenty from Everett.

But first she had to bring a halt to Kurt Slater's devious stealing. How could he do such a thing? He didn't seem like the devious type. Of course, she didn't really know him yet. No doubt he deteriorated on longer acquaintance. She only knew he was devastatingly handsome, and that she'd have to bear in mind at all times that she was dealing with a snake.

The man was definitely a charmer. How else had he persuaded Nancy Alton to help him rip off Everett's designs? But Shawna wouldn't let him charm her. Because she would never let herself forget that he was the enemy, the man who'd caused a world of sorrow in her life. Scowling at the redhead in the mirror, Shawna folded her arms defiantly. "By hook or by crook, I'm going to stop Kurt Slater!"

Chapter Two

In the morning Shawna awoke with a strange feeling. The hazy white sky and the sea tang in the air smelled home in Connecticut, but what had happened to her room? She should be facing the bookshelf that held her childhood collection of stuffed animals. She shook away the last wisps of sleep and sat up. Of course, Spindrift Cottage... and Kurt Slater. An image of his savage face popped into her head, lending a note of excitement to the day.

A glance at her watch told her it was eight-thirty. The omnipresent white haze of sky didn't fool her into thinking it was going to be a bad day. She knew the coastal weather. The sun seldom shone brightly, but it was there, squeezing through the mist, ready to burn you alive if you weren't careful.

She slipped on a robe and padded downstairs to the kitchen. While the coffee perked, she ran upstairs and dressed. A navy-and-white-striped T-shirt and white shorts were all she needed for a day at the beach. After she poured her coffee, she went to the window to see if Kurt was out. He was either a late sleeper or he was at work already. At least he wasn't outside.

She drank her coffee, ate a prune Danish and an apple. Then she went outside and walked along the beach, occasionally checking to see if Kurt was up and about. At about nine-thirty it occurred to her that the days were going to be very long if she didn't find something to do.

Back inside, she went upstairs and made her bed, tidied the kitchen, dusted the cottage and arranged her own belongings more comfortably. When the place was as homey as she could make it, she looked at the clock. It wasn't even ten o'clock yet!

The ocean lured her. Swimming? Too cold. Sailing? No boat. Wind surfing? She'd tried that last summer at home and loved it. There had to be a place that rented boards in the nearby resort area. She decided to drive into Wells Beach and see what she could find.

With her car window open, it was a pleasant drive into the seaside town. Shawna parked and walked along the main street to see what the place had to offer. There were a few restaurants, a movie theater, a hotel and a few quaint stores.

She strolled through a variety store, picking up a few things she needed. A couple of paperbacks and magazines seemed like a good idea, and some suntan lotion. Farther along the street, she found a stand selling fresh clams and lobsters. She knew she would enjoy some of them before she left Maine.

Her walk led inevitably to the beach. There she found a shop renting surfboards and Windsurfers. Delighted, Shawna retrieved her car and drove back to the shop. A laid-back, bearded shopkeeper helped her put the Windsurfer in the trunk and tie down the door so it wouldn't flap in the wind.

Eager to ride the wind, she drove straight back to the cottage. But before she changed into her bathing suit, she decided to call Everett and let him know of her progress.

"Is Slater there?" Everett asked eagerly.

"Yes, I met him last night. We'll be seeing a bit of each other."

"Not too much, I hope! He has quite a reputation with the ladies, Shawna."

"Don't worry! I'm not going to fall for the man that's trying to ruin you."

"I'm not sure I let you do the right thing to go there." Uncle Max's voice was laced with concern. "I keep thinking of Nancy.... You didn't work with Nancy Alton long enough to know her very well, but she was an eminently sensible woman. She was a lot more mature and experienced than you, my dear."

"Maybe she didn't realize what she was getting into. I'm forewarned, and forewarned means forearmed, right?"

"You sound like your mother. All right, do what you can, but don't take any risks on my account. I'd never forgive myself if anything happened to you."

"Hey, Slater's a thief, not a murderer." Shawna laughed.

"It's not murder that I'm worried about. It's a broken heart."

Shawna gave a cynical grin. "Now don't be a romantic, Everett."

"Keep in touch."

"I will. Bye for now."

It was nearly noon, and Shawna decided to have a sandwich before going to the beach. She poured a glass of milk and thumbed through a fashion magazine while eating. There was an article on the new designers. From the glossy page, she saw Kurt's eyes staring at her. They weren't as dark as she'd thought last night, in the moonlight. They were green.

She scanned quickly through the part of the article dealing with him. "The reclusive Slater shuns the spotlight," she read with amusement. The "recluse" was pictured attending a party in a white jacket, with a luscious blonde on his arm. Kurt was famous for his beautiful women. Reclusive? Shawna had her doubts.

Shawna shoved the magazine aside and changed into her sporty green maillot that fit like a second skin. The suit was plain, but as she was a serious swimmer, she liked its comfort. Outside, she hauled the unwieldy board to the ocean's edge, adjusted the sail and pushed the board out into the water. The temperature here seemed a lot colder than the Long Island Sound. Of course, it was farther north, and without the sheltering inlet. She hadn't seen many people actually swimming at Wells Beach, and most of the surfers wore rubber suits.

The fear of plunging into that icy water would be good incentive to keep afloat on her board. She climbed on, and before she even had the sail set to catch the wind, she was in the water. It felt like being plunged into an ice bath. A spontaneous howl of protest cut the air when she surfaced. One long lock of her hair streamed into her eyes, impeding her vision.

Before she had a chance to right the board, she was attacked by Brix. She hadn't seen the dog on the beach, and had no way of knowing that wind surfing was the Border collie's favorite sport, rating higher than digging up clams. The dog's sharp little claws scratched her arms as Shawna tried to push her away.

"Beat it, Brix. This is a human sport. No canines allowed."

Brix barked happily and clawed at the board. Her black plumed tail was wagging like a metronome set at double time. When Shawna finally got the board and sail righted, Brix clambered up before she got on herself. The dog's four paws clutched at the board, and her barrel chest was heaving with exertion. The determined gleam in her eyes showed she had no intention of leaving.

The blue-and-white sail caught the breeze, and within minutes Shawna was being wafted along the ocean. The sport that looked so graceful and effortless from land was, in fact, very taxing. Her arm muscles strained to keep the mast in line, and her legs were taut from balancing on the perilously moving board. It had taken her weeks of practice at home to master the delicate art, which depended as much on strength as skill and perseverance.

But it had been worth every minute of it. Shawna found it exhilarating to be single-handedly defying the raw elements of nature: the powerful, rolling ocean and the ocean winds. The Long Island Sound had been smoother going, but not as challenging as the open sea. The wind that billowed the sail also caught her hair and blew it across her face. Salt spray tingled on her tongue, and the rough water lapping over the board was ice-cold.

Shawna glanced behind her at Brix and was struck with the idea that the dog was smiling. Her wide mouth was open, and it seemed that she was adding her bit to the balancing act, leaning a little this way or that as the roll of the board indicated.

"Show off!" she called. Brix yelped happily.

Watching from his doorway, Kurt Slater was entranced by the sight. He had come out to call Brix, and when he saw the wind surfer, he knew where he'd find his dog. Brix would walk a mile over broken glass to get on a surfboard. The sun glinted on Shawna's coppery hair, and Kurt's eyes narrowed in speculation.

Wind surfing wasn't something you picked up in a morning. Shawna had obviously done it before. Of course she said last night she liked the ocean. She probably vacationed on the water whenever she got the chance. An anticipatory smile lit his face, and he dashed off. Within minutes, he had his board at the ocean's edge.

Sailing required all Shawna's attention. So she didn't know Kurt was even out of his cottage till his board skimmed alongside hers, his red-and-white sail billowing in the breeze. As he passed, his wide grin revealed dazzling white teeth. In spite of herself, Shawna felt a surge of pleasure. Racing was more fun than solo surfing.

It was impossible to talk over the singing of the wind, but when Kurt pointed toward the lighthouse at the end of the sound, she understood. The race was on. Brix barked in frustration. Her place was with her master, but as his board skimmed ahead, the dog knew it was impossible to overtake him. She barked a rallying encouragement at Shawna, the barks becoming more peremptory as they slipped farther behind.

Shawna felt the rush of competition, but surfing on the open ocean was new to her, and she didn't want the ignominy of falling into the sea. She looked ahead to check how widely Kurt was opening his sail to the strong wind. Instead, she found her eyes skimming over his back. The broad wedge of tanned muscles moved effortlessly. His proud head glinted in the hazy sunlight. Only his taut leg muscles, braced for control and balance, revealed any tension.

Brix's bark became positively irate as her master pulled ever farther ahead. In a final burst of frustration, the dog jumped into the ocean and began paddling. Shawna thought of stopping to rescue Brix, but the rugged, whale-shaped wedge of rock holding the lighthouse loomed close now, and Brix could swim to safety.

The next time she looked at Kurt, he was neatly swerving near the edge of the rock. He leaped from the Windsurfer to the rock in one smooth move, grabbing the mast to ease his vessel to safety. That was a new maneuver to Shawna.

Her arrival was less graceful. She turned the sail to slow her progress and found herself floundering two yards from the rock. Kurt came to the edge and held out a hand to help her as she glided shoreward. His strong arm steadied her, and when she leaped from the board, he caught the end of it. Kurt showed her where the rock ledge tapered out to allow easier landing farther inland.

"Not bad for a beginner!" he complimented her. "I guess you've done this before."

"Never with a stowaway dog," she said with a laugh. "Where *is* Brix?"

"She'll be here, never fear."

Looking across the water, they spotted Brix's nose and ears, and a frenzied whir of paws as she paddled toward them. As Shawna arranged her Windsurfer on the beach, Kurt rescued the tired dog from the water. On shore, Brix shook herself, scattering water in all directions. When this important detail had been attended to, she ran off to explore the island.

"What is this place? Is there anything to see?" Shawna asked.

"Just the lighthouse, but it isn't even manned nowadays. It's computerized."

"Computers, even in a place like this. It seems a desecration."

"Maybe computer is the wrong word. It's automatic anyway. There's really nothing here but rock, rock, and more rock. A great place for sunning. Sometimes I come over here, just to be alone."

The rock was uneven, rising to modest heights in some places before falling to valleys, where sea water was trapped. They clambered over the rough surface toward the end of the little peninsula.

"Where'd you learn to wind surf like that?" Kurt asked.

"During my vacation in Cape Cod last year," she said glibly, having anticipated the question. "I'm out of practice. I'll have to polish my style a little before I challenge you to another race."

Kurt had mounted a peak of rock. He looked down at her and grinned. "No, you'll have to polish it a *lot*. I was holding back to give you a chance."

He spoke jokingly, but the arrogant boast pricked Shawna's pride. He looked like the king of the castle, standing on that rock peak, enjoying his supremacy. She could see that he was competitive—so competitive he'd do anything to win?

She gave a dismissing shrug. "I'm not really into competition." But she instinctively looked around for a higher peak to climb, and was soon looking down on him.

"So I noticed," he said, and laughed knowingly. "Race you to the top of the lighthouse. That's a joke!"

Instead, they strolled out to the point of rock beyond the white tower. Before them, the ocean swelled ominously, moistening the black rock edged with a slippery green growth.

"It's very deep here," Kurt mentioned.

"It can't be. They don't put lighthouses in deep water. They're used to warn boaters from rocks."

"It's deep at this end. The rocks are like submerged mountains here—high and low levels. The shallow area that's dangerous for shipping is on the other side, where we landed."

It even angered Shawna that he was the expert, though he'd lived here all his life. What was it about this man that ignited all her antagonistic electricity? It would seem not only petty but ridiculous to challenge him about the rocks, so she found another subject.

"Brix is annoying the sea gulls," she pointed out. The dog appeared to be in a fight with three large gulls over a fish that had washed up on the rocks.

Kurt gave her a haughty, questioning look. "That's one way of putting it. I'd say the sea gulls are annoying Brix. She had the fish first." He whistled, and Brix came running, leaving the birds to argue over the fish.

"You know, Shawna, you're a poor loser."

"I haven't had much practice at losing," she retaliated.

Kurt just smiled lazily. She looked at him, and found herself drowning in his eyes. Their color, an indeterminate grayish-green, unfathomably deep and dangerous, reminded her of the sea. "Don't tempt me," he said. Some atavistic instinct that he realized was not at all gentlemanly urged him to put this woman into line. A little slip of a girl weighing about a hundred pounds shouldn't be so pugnacious.

"Tempt you to what?"

"To teach you how to lose more gracefully. Isn't that what we're talking about?"

She cast a taunting smile at him. "You're an expert at losing, are you?"

Kurt gave a dismissing shrug. "I've had my share of failures. I don't take losing very well myself."

"Then you're hardly the one to teach me failure with grace, are you?"

He bowed with mock formality. "I acquiesce to your superior logic, Miss Cassidy. I can't teach you to fail—gracefully, I mean. I can only provide the opportunity for you to learn."

She knew he meant to teach her a lesson all the same, and within two minutes he set about doing it.

"Not much to do here. Shall we go back to the cottage?" he asked.

"Sure."

Kurt leaped ahead, scrambling up and down rocks to the Windsurfers, with Brix yapping at his heels. He steadied his board, climbed on and was soon skimming homeward across the bay. Only Brix looked back and barked a friendly farewell.

Shawna's temper was smoldering at being left behind. She found it very hard to mount her board from the rock ledge. The uneven footing sent her slipping and sliding, and before she got afloat, she had endured not one but two dunks in the cold ocean. Her hair streamed in her eyes, annoying her. But most annoying of all was the sight of Kurt skimming effortlessly away, beating her by a mile.

Her anger wasn't assuaged when he hauled in his sail and waited for her, but she quelled it. She had to keep on superficially friendly terms with him. She needed to get access to his sketches, to get into his cottage, and she wouldn't accomplish that by pouting.

"I'm a quick learner," she called across the water, as she approached him. "See how gracefully I'm losing?" She even managed a stiff-lipped smile.

They coasted onto shore side by side, and Kurt helped her haul in her board. "You shouldn't stay out too long the first day," he warned her. "It doesn't look as if there's any sun, but don't let the haze fool you. With your complexion, you could get badly burned." He used it as an excuse to examine her.

"More likely freckled," she said, wrinkling her nose.

Shawna felt acutely conscious of her freckled face and body as Kurt's sea-green eyes roved over her. The closeness of his observation made her feel vulnerable. Her skimpy suit fit like spray paint. Her hair was wet and windblown, and no doubt even this much exposure to the sun had darkened her freckles.

"That's better than a burn, isn't it?" he said. The timbre of his voice revealed an underlying tension. Kurt found himself peculiarly attracted to this unglamorous sea urchin. She was too thin, and she was bad tempered. She'd hardly said a civil word to him since he met her, and yet he wanted to take her into his arms and kiss those sulky, pouting lips.

"Easy for you to say," she scowled, looking at his perfectly tanned body. Kurt stood, arms akimbo, in a macho pose designed to infuriate her. He wasn't even breathing hard after swooping across the bay and hauling in two Windsurfers.

"Why don't you throw something over your shoulders, and we'll go beachcombing?" he suggested.

"Sure," she agreed, but reluctantly. She'd been hoping to get into his cottage. "I'll be right back."

Shawna darted into the cottage and grabbed her beach coat. She'd designed and sewed it herself as a project in design school. It had a flared back and a big hood that could be used to protect your head in the sun. The lining was white terry cloth, but the outside was a flamboyant riot of colors.

"You won't be hard to recognize in that, if I happen to see you a few miles down the beach." He smiled. Her scowl told him she'd read a slur into it. "It's cute," he added, to appease her.

The style was good. He liked the extravagant sweep of the full back. Kurt instinctively lifted the hood to see the garment's possibilities. He took the material between his fingers, testing its texture, and lifted it over her head. Her fire-bright hair stood out against the white lining. "It's really interesting," he murmured unthinkingly.

He would have emphasized the drama of the flared design by using an unpatterned material, but maybe the bright colors were better for casual wear.

Shawna's breath stopped in her lungs as he assessed her design. She found she was inordinately interested in his opinion. Her eyes glittered as he went on, twitching at the hood, even looking at the seams.

Maybe this was her chance to prod him into a confession. "You sound like a designer or something," she said.

A conscious, guilty look flashed across Kurt's face. His hands fell, and he turned away. "I just like nice things," he said nonchalantly. He soon turned back to her and added in a more intimate tone, "Especially when a pretty girl's wearing them."

Had he noticed that the coat was handmade? "My Mom made this for me. She'll be flattered that you like it," she said, and began walking along the beach.

"Oh, is she a seamstress?" Kurt asked.

"No, she just makes some of our clothes."

As they passed Kurt's cottage, Shawna said, "I hope I'm not keeping you from your work."

"I always take either the morning or afternoon off. I often work at night. There's not much else to do here in the evening."

"You promised to show me some of your illustrations," she reminded him.

"I'll do better than that. I'll do a sketch of you sometime."

"Sometime" was too vague to suit her, so she made a great fuss about it to hurry things along. "Really! That'd be neat. Why don't you do it now?"

"Because now we're collecting driftwood for my fireplace," he said. "There's a nice big piece up ahead."

They ran along the beach and Shawna helped him drag a gnarled and weathered piece of tree trunk to his woodpile. Brix helped by running in and out between their legs and barking.

Kurt's woodpile was at his back door. "Don't we get rewarded by a drink or something?" she hinted.

"Name your poison. I've got beer and iced tea."

"Iced tea, if it's homemade, and with real lemon."

"What other kind is there?" he asked, opening the door for her to enter.

They passed through a woodshed, well stocked with driftwood, into the kitchen. Shawna fell in love with the kitchen at first sight. It was huge, with a wood stove in one corner. The floor was tiled in black-and-white squares like an enormous chessboard. A well-worn pine table and chairs occupied one end of the room. On the table a bouquet of wildflowers in a blue-and-white jug added a touch of summer. The flowers were simple daisies and buttercups and purple vetch, but the arrangement looked charming.

All the modern conveniences of refrigerator, stove, dishwasher and even a microwave oven had been added, but the room was big enough that they didn't appear incongruous. On one stark white wall there was a collection of old iron hardware: a pair of two-foot ice tongs, sheep slippers, old tools and farm implements, all artistically arranged. It was a cheerful, friendly room, obviously arranged by someone who loved the kitchen and considered it more than a workplace.

"This is lovely, Kurt," she said.

"Thanks. I don't know if Mom'd approve of what I've done with it. We had those tools and things in a shed out back. I needed the space for a garage, and I kind of hated to part with the old junk, so I hung it in here."

So it was Kurt's taste she was admiring. And Kurt who had picked those wildflowers and put them in the pretty old milk pitcher. How strange to think of the dashing Kurt Slater harboring this sentimental streak.

He handed her a glass of iced tea, topped with a slice of lemon, and took a can of beer for himself. "Let's go out to the porch where it's more comfortable," he suggested.

Shawna looked around the living room as they passed through. Its general setup was familiar to her. What she was looking for was evidence. She noticed there was no sketch on the drawing board now. He'd been careful to put it away. Her eyes slid to a row of built-in cabinets along the far wall. That could be where he kept his sketches.

"I thought you were doing your illustrations this morning. I don't see them," she said, making it a casual inquiry.

"I took the finished one to the post office," he said, and opened the door to the porch.

Apparently familiar with this routine, Brix was already curled up in one of the chairs. They sat in the shade with their feet propped on the porch banister.

"This is the life," Shawna said, sipping her iced tea.

"It beats pounding a typewriter in an office, huh?"

"Yeah," she agreed, feeling a twinge of guilt. But why should she? He was lying, too.

Shawna stared out at the endlessly rolling ocean, retreating into infinity. Swell followed swell, breaking on the shore with a muted crash, leaving a ripple of curdled foam behind. "It makes you feel kind of insignificant," she said pensively.

"Maybe that's why I love it so much. It's a great place to keep your life in perspective. In the general scheme of things, one man is about as significant as a grain of sand on this beach."

She peered at him curiously. "You need that kind of reminder, do you? You sound as though life has gone to your head or something. Are you so famous, Kurt?" she teased.

Kurt came within a heartbeat of telling her who he was. He considered his answer before speaking, hating to interrupt the smooth advance of their friendship. But Shawna's flippant lack of respect was a pleasant change, and she might start behaving like the others if he told her the truth.

"I can hardly claim to be famous when you don't recognize me," he parried. "But my work's becoming known in my own field," he admitted modestly. "I guess I could say I'm successful, not famous. I make pretty good money, if that's any criterion. I have the respect of my colleagues."

Shawna's jaws moved silently. *That's what you think!*

Kurt continued talking, in a contemplative mood as he stared at the ocean. One hand thoughtlessly stroked Brix's head. "More important than any of that—fame or money—is the satisfaction of doing good work. Creative work is very rewarding."

Shawna had to admit that he put on a very convincing act. Modest, unassuming—and a liar. Creative work, my eye. Creative theft. Her blood simmered to see him so satisfied, so smug, enjoying all the rewards without doing the work. What surprised her was that he didn't brag more. Why didn't he tell her who he was?

Meanwhile she had to say something, or he might become suspicious. "Everybody needs a creative outlet," she said idly. "I write poetry."

Kurt turned toward her, smiling in interest. "Oh really! I love poetry. What kind do you write? Modern, free verse or what?"

"Romantic poetry. I like Keats, Shelley, Wordsworth."

"I've never been much good at writing. I kept a diary once, for a year or so, but it was so dull I gave it up."

"Dull!" The word exploded out of her mouth before she realized it. Kurt Slater's life was about as dull as dynamite.

"The way I wrote it, it was dull." He laughed. "As I said, I'm not much good with words. I think in pictures. What fascinates me is how some people think in terms of music. Can you imagine Mozart or Beet-

hoven having all that beautiful music in his head?
Where does it come from?''

They ended up talking about the mystery of cre-
ativity. It was easy to be lured into this seductive subject, in the never-never atmosphere of the ocean. The
water swelled and rolled virtually at their doorstep,
making them aware that they were at the edge of the
continent, with no intrusion from society. Just the
waves and wind and sea gulls. For an hour and a half
they talked about their favorite music and books and
paintings, without agreeing on anything. It intrigued
Shawna that Kurt didn't monopolize the conversation the way most successful men did. Like Everett,
for instance. Kurt seemed genuinely interested in
Shawna's views.

It was a strange, unreal afternoon. Time seemed to
stand still, or be irrelevant, as they talked. When Kurt
went to get them another drink, Shawna followed him
to the door and glanced around the living room for
other possible hiding places. But with Brix wagging
her tail behind her, she knew this wasn't the moment
for a search. And really she didn't feel like interrupt-
ing the languorous mood that had crept over her.

It had been a long time since she had spent a quiet
afternoon just talking to someone, getting to know
him. And this was the last man she would have chosen for the experience. She didn't want to know that
Kurt Slater had feelings. She didn't want to hear that
he admired his parents, that he phoned them every
Friday evening at seven, no matter where he was, and
always flew south for their birthdays.

And she especially didn't like the way her insides
melted whenever he smiled in approval at her made-up

confessions. She hated that she'd manufactured a whole life for herself, withholding the confidences he'd shared so generously. She shouldn't stay for another glass of iced tea. Kurt shouldn't have insisted she try it with lime, *his* way. He shouldn't have caressed her with his sea-deep eyes and told her he didn't share his culinary secrets with just anyone.

She should get up right now and say she had to dash back to Spindrift Cottage and—sit alone, wishing she were back here with him. But she couldn't see him again. This wasn't the way to search his cottage. She would have to wait at home watching for him to leave. Then she'd sneak in. She had noticed his back door wasn't locked. So trusting . . .

Just as Kurt came out with her new drink, a bell sounded on the road behind the cottage. It was an old-fashioned sound, like a school bell.

"That'll be Charlie," Kurt said. "He delivers fresh lobster. You're going to love the way I broil them."

So she was staying for dinner then. A reluctant smile lifted her lips.

Chapter Three

If you're using a tablecloth, I'm going home to change," Shawna announced when Kurt began arranging the table for dinner.

He looked over his shoulder from the drawer where he was choosing a cloth. "I kind of like what you're wearing," he said. His eyes flickered over the skimpy green suit, and Shawna felt a definite mushiness invade her insides. "Does that mean I have to change as well?" he asked.

It was on the tip of her tongue to say she liked what he was wearing, too. Those brief, fringed jeans didn't leave much to the imagination. Especially when they began slipping down over his lean stomach, revealing that line of white skin.

Kurt hadn't touched her all afternoon, not once. He'd almost seemed to go out of his way not to touch her hand when he'd handed her each drink. Imagination proved very effective, however. She could imagine all too readily how his taut, tanned chest and arms would feel against her.

"I hope you're going to put on a shirt at least," she said.

"Don't worry, my mother taught me the basics of civilized behavior. She always threatened me and Dad that if we came to the table topless, she'd do the same. You go on and change, while I prepare the lobsters."

"I'll be glad to miss the execution," she admitted.

"Dinner will be ready in half an hour."

Shawna scooted out the door and ran all the way to Spindrift Cottage, not because she had to hurry, but because she felt happily excited. She knew she should be nervous at the anticipation of the evening, but giddy happiness repeatedly bubbled over, destroying her objectivity.

What should she wear? Kurt had put candles on the table. She wanted to wear something floating and romantic—even a flower in her hair—but this was casual cottage country, and she shouldn't overdo it.

She took a quick shower to get rid of the ocean's sand and salt water. After some thought, she compromised on a sleeveless tank top and a full skirt that came midway down her calf. The striped skirt was edged in eyelet style embroidery, and she wore a starched petticoat under it to make it stand out. It rustled romantically when she walked. Her hair flamed like the setting sun as she brushed it back. Her freckles were dark from the sun, but the rest of her skin had taken on a pinkish glow, so she didn't look too bad.

On impulse, she sprayed a light flowery cologne behind her ears and on her neck. She grabbed a bottle of sauterne and was halfway out the door before she remembered that she hadn't worn any jewelry. Her big white hoop earrings would look good with this outfit, she thought, dashing back to the bedroom. *Concentrate on remaining objective,* she reminded herself. This might be the night she discovered where Kurt kept his designs.

Brix ran out to meet her and escorted her to the door. The dog's bark brought Kurt to greet them. He had changed into a striped sport shirt and faded tan trousers that clung to his hips and hugged his muscled thighs. His hair was combed back with water, which she knew wouldn't last long.

"My contribution," she said, handing him the wine.

"Thanks, but you didn't have to bring anything. I've already opened wine. We'll have this some other time."

"I thought your beverages were limited to tea and beer."

An appreciative smile hovered on his lips as he examined her outfit. Shawna had the knack of looking terrific in simple clothes, but he instinctively imagined what he'd design for her. She'd probably dislike anything frilly, but he'd like to see her in some of his high-fashion designs.

"Those are my afternoon drinks," he said. "In the evening, I splurge and serve wine, to my very special guests." Shawna felt her body blossom with pleasure at the compliment.

They went into the kitchen, where white china and pistol-handled cutlery were arranged on a deep-blue linen cloth. It looked simple but elegant, just the right style for Kurt, she thought. The dishes weren't fine china, and the cutlery was stainless steel, but the wineglasses were cut crystal. Prisms of light reflected in their deeply etched pattern, tracing an abstract spectrum on the cloth.

The wine was very good. Shawna sneaked a glance at the French label as he poured. The salad was a simple mélange of various greens, topped with split endives. The bitter taste of escarole played off well against the milder Boston lettuce and romaine. Kurt's own dressing of olive oil, lemon juice and spices lent a piquant dash to the dish. Fresh French bread and the broiled lobster completed their meal. Shawna had never tasted anything so delicious and was lavish in her praise.

"The trick is to clarify the butter, not just melt it," he explained.

"I think the trick is to have fresh lobster."

"That goes without saying!"

As they pried the succulent lobster meat from its shell, Kurt smiled nostalgically. "You know, it's kind of funny. When I was growing up, the poorer kids took lobster sandwiches to school, because we could catch it free. Now it's considered a gourmet item. My mom and dad won't touch it these days, but I still have it often. I just happen to like it."

"Were you poor?" Shawna asked, and found herself mentally excusing his treachery of stealing Everett's designs.

He looked around the comfortable house. "We never had much cash to spare, though I never thought of us as actually poor. At least we had plenty to eat.

Kids don't miss not having a new bike and fancy clothes if their home life is good. Mine was good, very good."

"I think you said your dad was a cabinetmaker?"

"Yes, but he did plain carpentry and repairs, too, to make ends meet. He also fished a little. He made most of the furniture in this house. How about your folks?"

Shawna couldn't tell him her mother was Adele. He might recognize the name, and connect her with Everett. "My dad sold insurance," she said. "It wasn't really a lie, she consoled herself. Her dad had sold insurance, before he was made district sales manager for the company.

"The same company you work for?"

"Yes."

"You mentioned your mom made your clothes."

"Yes," she admitted, feeling like a traitor. Shawna was quick to change the subject. "Where's Brix?"

"Probably out digging clams. She won't go far from home. I hope she didn't frighten you last night."

"She did, actually."

"It's odd that she decided to pester you. She doesn't usually bother anyone unless they invade her space—which is *my* space. She knows exactly where her boundaries are. Sure you weren't trespassing?" he asked with a smile.

It was intriguing to see small flames of the candlelight reflect in the sea of his eyes. The water on his hair had dried, and one sun-bleached lock was beginning to fall forward. "Maybe I set foot on your beach," she answered nervously. "I'm a newcomer. I wasn't sure of the boundaries."

"Hey, I was just kidding," he said. "We're all friendly here. There are no boundaries."

He noticed her wineglass was empty, and filled it again. The wine was a pale, wheaty shade, very dry, and very good.

"You have to have another lobster," he urged. "I have two more broiling in the oven. They weren't very big."

"I don't think I could. I won't have any room for dessert."

"There isn't any dessert!" he exclaimed, and looked shocked at his own negligence. "That was thoughtless of me! I should have bought something. I have some grapes if you . . ."

Shawna smiled. "It doesn't matter. I'd really rather have another lobster, if you're sure it's small."

"Next time I'll have dessert. What do you like? No, let me guess! Something with whipped cream and flaky pastry. There's a bakery in Wells Beach that makes fantastic French pastries."

Shawna heard herself say, "Next time it's my turn." Now where had that invitation come from? Years of socializing had trained her in the niceties of polite entertaining, and she knew she should repay Kurt's hospitality. But she was falling in too deep. She already liked him more than she should.

He was so darned easy to like! That was the trouble. As she glanced across the table at him, she knew he'd be just as easy to love. Shawna had stopped thinking of his face as savage. It was a handsome, interesting face. His high cheekbones were fascinating, and those mobile, expressive eyebrows that had looked almost artistically phony last night just suited the drama of his face. They were the perfect frame for his devastating eyes.

"What's your specialty?" he asked. "It wouldn't be seafood, when you live in Lewiston. Steak? Roast beef? Hamburgers?"

"I can do better than burgers," she said, scanning her mind for a gourmet dish that she would serve him.

"Don't go to any trouble. I'm easy. To please, I mean. I mean, food-wise..." He stopped and laughed. Why was he stuttering like a damned adolescent?

"I get the idea, Kurt." She smiled.

An answering smile softened his savage face. He lifted his glass and touched hers. When he spoke, his voice was low-pitched and intimate. "When it comes to women, I'm afraid I'm not so easy to please. But I haven't met anyone who pleases me as much as you for a long time."

Shawna found herself unable to meet his gaze. A worm of discontent curled inside her. Was this a line he was pitching her? She sure hoped so. "You call that hard to please?" she asked, in a careless voice. "I'm not even pretty. I'm skinny, redhaired and freckled."

"You're willowy, Titian haired and polka dotted," he said, a mischievous twinkle sparkling in his eyes. "Besides, I just happen to like red hair and freckles. But I wasn't talking about your looks. I like your—inner beauty," he said, choosing the words carefully. "You seem like—oh, I don't know. I told you I was no good with words. You don't seem as spoiled and arti-ficial as other women. You're natural, and honest. You're easy to talk to, Shawna."

She was feeling worse by the minute. "Honest" seemed like a bad joke, considering her motives for being here. And what did he want with an honest woman, anyway? Did he find that kind easier to fool? Barely controlling her confused anger, she said demurely, "I admire honesty, too, Kurt."

"Shall we drink to that?" he suggested, lifting his glass. Shawna's fingers were unsteady as she raised hers and lightly clinked it against his. The crystal emitted a clear, bell-like tinkle that hung on the air, mocking their toast.

They had their coffee on the front porch. "So Brix won't be too jealous," Kurt explained. "She's used to having me more to herself. She pulls the comforter and pillows off my bed when she gets jealous."

"I thought you'd use patchwork quilts," Shawna said, and felt a flush grow at her revelation. She shouldn't have told him she'd been thinking about his bed.

Kurt didn't make any vulgar comment about the direction of her thoughts. "Since I make my own bed, I've switched to a comforter—easier to make," he explained, and went on with the conversation. "Do you ride, Shawna?"

"No, I've never had the opportunity to learn."

"It's too bad you're leaving so soon. I keep my horse at a stable down the road. They have horses for hire, too. It's exhilarating to gallop along the beach, early in the morning, with the spindrift blowing off the ocean. It's a great way to start the day."

"It sounds lovely," she sighed. The image of it sharpened in her mind: galloping along beside Kurt, watching the sun come up. "But I couldn't learn to gallop in one week, and I guess walking along the beach wouldn't be much fun for you."

"Maybe you could try it, anyway. Lewiston's not that far away, you know. No reason you couldn't come down and visit me some weekend."

A weekend alone with Kurt? It would be sheer heaven—and quite impossible. Shawna didn't notice she hadn't answered till Kurt prodded her. "Or is there a special man in Lewiston?" he asked. His green eyes were bright with interest.

"No! It's not that."

He nodded, satisfied with the vehemence of her denial. "I get it. You're scared stiff of horseback riding, but your competitive pride won't let you say so. There's an easy solution."

In her mind, Shawna set herself seated behind Kurt, her arms wrapped around his waist as he galloped along the beach. The horse was a well-muscled chestnut, with a flying mane.

"A dune buggy," he announced. "I succumbed to a lifelong temptation and got myself one for my birthday last month. It's totally impractical and childish. I love it. Tomorrow morning?" he suggested. "About seven? Dawn's the best time. I'll even spring for breakfast after."

She was getting in too deep. She knew she should say no. The earliness of the hour provided a good enough excuse. She was on vacation; she didn't want to get up at the crack of dawn. But when she looked at his expectant face, with a smile ready to break, she said, "It sounds lovely." As a sop, she told herself it would make a good excuse to leave early tonight.

"Your chauffeur will be at your door at seven."

Bored with their conversation, Brix went off to roam along the beach. "If you're providing breakfast as well as dinner, the least I can do is clean up your kitchen," Shawna volunteered.

They went inside. Shawna cleared the table while Kurt stacked the dishwasher. The great playboy Slater, stacking a dishwasher! It seemed so natural, working side by side with him. He wasn't turning out to be the kind of man she thought he was at all. He wasn't proud or macho or aggressive. Was it possible Everett was wrong about him? It did seem strange that Kurt never mentioned his real job. Why was he pretending that he was a commercial illustrator?

When the kitchen was clean, they carried cups of coffee into the living room. "You were going to show me some of your work," Shawna reminded him.

"No, I was going to do a sketch of you. Now let me see." Kurt stood back and studied her. "I want you with the lamplight playing off your hair. This'll take a while. Why don't you pile those pillows up behind you and get comfortable? But don't fall asleep. I want to capture that peculiar shade of your eyes. Darker than peridots, but brighter than emeralds." As he gazed at her, a feeling of tension grew.

"Green as grass?" Shawna suggested facetiously, to control the mood.

"I was going to say grass, but I was wrong. They're beer-bottle green." Kurt lifted one finger and touched her nose. "And a cute little button nose."

Even the touch of one finger had an effect on Shawna's calm sense of control. Or maybe it was the admiring way he was examining her, his eyes lingering on her eyes, the curve of her cheek, her lips.... "Beer bottles and buttons. This is going to be some portrait," she said. "I didn't know you were into surrealism."

"I'm not." Kurt pointed to the sofa and Shawna began arranging pillows. "I'm not skilled enough to paint a real portrait," he told her. "This is only a sketch. I don't expect you to dash out and have it framed."

He went to his drafting board and turned it so that he could sketch while facing her. Shawna watched to see if he went to the cabinets for his equipment. If they were locked, that'd look suspicious. But Kurt didn't have to go to the cabinets; there were charcoal pencils and pastels resting on the ledge of his board. A pad of drawing paper was already in place as well.

Before Kurt took up a charcoal, he examined Shawna's pose. "There's not enough light," he said, and went to adjust the lamp so it shone on her. When the light was right, he stood with his head cocked to one side, assessing her pose.

"We need more pillows," he said, picking up a large cushion from the end of the sofa. "Right about here," he said, slipping his hand beneath her head to insert the pillow. His fingers felt disturbingly warm against her neck, and his breath fanned her cheek. At this close range, she could see the individual lashes that shadowed his eyes. When he looked up, she was smote with his deep green-gray gaze.

It was a peculiarly impersonal look. When Kurt sketched, his mind was on his work, period. The same professional approach was there when he brushed the long lock of hair back from her forehead, but even his impersonal touch stirred an excitement in her. She caught a whiff of soap, minty and sweet, from his skin. Slater, with his own line of perfume, didn't even wear an after-shave. Shawna decided he must have a split personality. This couldn't be the same man who attended all the New York premieres and extravaganzas with gorgeous models on his arm.

Kurt gave the pillow a final pat and went to his drafting board. He studied her for a long moment, then picked up his charcoal. His hand moved swiftly, surely, as he sketched in the lineaments of her head. A proud little head, he thought. Her unusual haircut showed a streak of individuality. And the fact that she didn't try to camouflage her freckles with makeup told him she wasn't vain.

In fact, as far as he could tell, Shawna didn't wear any makeup except lipstick. She wasn't flirtatious or forward, but she wasn't a shy violet, either. She knew her own mind and spoke it. He caught the arch of her neck and drew in her shoulders. He would have to sketch only the head and shoulders, or else he'd be working all night.

A smile curved his sensuous lips as he worked. The sketch was going perfectly. Maybe because this particular face had been in his mind for twenty-four hours, just waiting to be captured on paper. On paper? This one was worth capturing in the flesh. What a relief to be with a woman who wasn't eternally looking in her mirror, or worrying that her fingernails were coming off, or complaining that she couldn't eat or else she would get fat. Fat! The models were all skin and bone. Of course, that was a requirement for their work. Designers didn't want a voluptuous figure interfering with the lines and contours of their creations.

He liked her competitive streak, too. Shawna wasn't a woman who would sit and bask in the reflected glory of her husband. She would live her own life. He felt lucky that she liked the beach—but would she enjoy living in New York? Of course, it was early to be thinking in terms of a commitment, but he hadn't met anyone else who had seriously interested him for a long time. After just twenty-four hours, he felt he could come to love Shawna Cassidy. Maybe it was time to discover if she felt anything for him.

The outline was finished, and he began selecting colors to give form and body to the sketch. Pastels were the wrong medium to catch the leaping flames of her hair. Even oils would be inadequate. He shaded in orange and gold and a few streaks of red to give the general effect. Then he selected two green pencils to do her eyes. She hadn't been flattered at that "beer-bottle green" description. It was the right color, though, when the sun shone through an empty bottle. The fringe of black lashes lent depth and distinction to her eyes. Biting back a smile, he liberally dotted on freckles over the bridge of her little button nose.

Shawna sat patiently, holding her pose like a professional. Her eyes never left Kurt as he worked. She was engrossed by his intensity. As she watched him, she could tell that he loved sketching. Maybe he was a thwarted artist? But he didn't seem like a thwarted anything. He was completely infatuated with his work ... and his model. There was definitely approval in those lingering glances as he assessed her features.

When Kurt was finished, he wrote Slater, in a bold hand across the bottom. "All done," he said, and ripped the sheet from the pad to show her.

Shawna reached eagerly for it. A gasp of delight caught in her throat. "This isn't me!" she exclaimed. He had transformed her red-haired freckled face into the mask of some enchanting nymph, sultrily gazing up from the corner of her eyes. Well, from where he stood, maybe the angle was right, but the rest of it was sheer flattery. She wasn't that pretty. He had made her eyes starrier, her smile sweeter; the whole pose an innocent provocation. The fact that he didn't bother drawing any clothes on her might cause that feeling. She didn't even notice the freckles, designed to annoy her.

Of course, it was only a head and shoulders portrait, and that was odd. You'd think a fashion designer would be more interested in the clothes.

"Shall I get a mirror? I think it's pretty accurate," he insisted, and sat beside her.

Shawna looked at him and shook her head. "Flattery will get you nowhere, Mr. Slater. I'm not this pretty. And where's my shirt?"

"Oh, did I forget it?" he asked, surprised to see it was missing. "I didn't want to get into drawing clothes, or we'd be here all night. Do you like it?"

"No, I love it. May I keep it?"

He bowed his head grandly. "Be my guest. Of course, I'll expect some payment," he added, with a wicked smile.

Shawna felt a jolt of alarm. Now it was coming. He was going to make a move on her. "What did you have in mind?" she asked warily.

His answering grin told her he understood her thinking. "Your turn to get us a drink, while I wash up. These pastels stick to your fingers."

Her alarm dwindled to pleasure. "Beer?" she asked.

"That's my nightcap. Get yourself whatever you want, bearing in mind my limited bar."

Kurt went to wash his hands, and Shawna suddenly found herself alone in the living room. This was her chance to try the cupboards, and for a change, Brix wasn't even around. She put the sketch aside and tiptoed to the row of cabinets along the far wall. She was unhappy to do it. It seemed treacherous to treat a gracious host so badly.

But when she discovered the cabinets were locked, her sense of wrongdoing faded and steely determination replaced it. Where would he keep the key? She looked around the room, but there wasn't time to search now. At least she knew where he kept anything that might incriminate him. Why would he bother locking the cabinets if there was nothing important in them?

She hurried into the kitchen and got two beers from the refrigerator. Above the sink, there was a ring of keys hanging on a hook. When Kurt returned, she was back on the sofa, smiling.

"I've had a lovely evening, Kurt. Thanks for the lobster—and the drawing."

"Thank you for your company. You didn't give me an answer about coming down some weekend. Is it our being alone here that bothers you? You could bring a friend—that girl who was supposed to join you for your vacation...."

Shawna was glad it had occurred to him that their spending a weekend alone together might dismay her. But what could she say now? "I'd have to see when she can get away."

"I hope it's soon. I could always shanghai some local woman to chaperon us. Not that it's really necessary. There are three bedrooms—with locks."

Shawna felt a warm flush creep up her neck. "My mother's kind of old-fashioned about that sort of thing," she said.

"I wouldn't want to ruin your reputation in Lewiston. Hey, how about bringing your mother along? Would she come?"

Things were going from bad to worse. Lying didn't come easily to Shawna, and she was beginning to find it particularly distasteful to lie to Kurt. She reminded herself of the locked cabinet. Only that suspicious evidence gave her the nerve to keep misleading him. "She'll be visiting her sister in Chicago for a few weeks. They get together every summer. Maybe we can arrange something later."

"Not too much later, I hope." His smile was encouraging. "I have no objections to visiting Lewiston, if it comes to that, but I was looking forward to having you here."

"We still have a week to go. Why don't we wait and see if you change your mind? You may find you tire of me easily."

Kurt held his can of beer just below his chin, gazing at her over the rim. "Somehow, I don't think that's going to happen, Shawna. And besides, we may not have a whole week. I have to be away on business a few days myself. But maybe I can postpone it." He lifted the can and took a long drink.

Shawna watched, fascinated, as the ridge in his throat moved up and down. A silence fell, and she said, "Why don't we put on some music?"

"I'll have to buy some Chopin, since you don't care for my composers." Kurt put on an instrumental tape, and they sat companionably, listening and drinking and talking.

The uncomfortable subject of her visit was left behind. It was of the immediate future that they discussed, planning picnics and rides in the dune buggy and wind surfing. It sounded like an idyllic vacation. If she'd sat down and planned every detail, it couldn't have been better. Except that she wouldn't be here in Maine scheming to expose Kurt's thievery. And he wouldn't be a pirate designer, masquerading as a commercial illustrator.

Why didn't he tell her who he was? He had no idea she worked for Everett. He couldn't know she suspected him. Why wasn't he boasting about being the great Slater? And since he obviously liked her, why didn't he kiss her?

When her drink was gone, Shawna said, "I'd better be getting home now. Thanks again, for everything."

"I'll walk you to your door. If we sneak out the front way real quietly, Brix might not hear. She sleeps out in the back in summer."

Shawna thought he was joking until he opened the front door with extreme caution. It didn't prevent Brix from picking up their scent and barking raucously as they left.

"She's worse than a suspicious wife." Shawna laughed.

"Let's call a spade a spade. She's a bitch."

"And you love her."

"I'm strongly attached to her. I reserve love for human friends."

Kurt took her hand and they strolled along the beach. The breeze caught her skirt and it billowed flirtatiously around her knees, the edge of white eyelet mimicking the lacy foam of the lapping waves. The moisture-laden air felt soft against her skin. She was becoming accustomed to the briny sea tang, like a familiar balm. The moon was invisible, but its presence above the clouds caused a strange luminescence, like a pearly mist.

"Riding at night is nice, too," Kurt said. "You've got to learn to ride, Shawna. I'll talk to the lady at the stables and see if she has a gentle horse."

The future could be so wonderful, if only... "You just want me to fall and make a fool of myself," she teased.

Kurt slipped his arm around her waist and pulled her closely against his hip. "I wouldn't let anything happen to you. I'd never forgive myself."

Again that warm feeling, stronger than contentment, swelled inside her. "Be sure you tell my horse that. You probably talk to the animals. You seem to have interesting conversations with Brix."

"You make me sound like some kind of nature freak."

It was a foolish conversation, one that suited their mood. The veiled moon and the isolated beach lent an eerie, unreal mood to their stroll. It wasn't a time for dull old common sense. When they reached Spindrift Cottage, Kurt sat on the balcony railing and linked his arms loosely around Shawna.

"Do I get a good-night kiss?" he asked.

The moment had finally come, and Shawna braced herself for it. She looped her arms around his neck and gave him a light, playful kiss on the cheek. When she began to pull back, his arms tightened around her and he moved his head to catch her mouth.

"We can do better than that," he murmured, just before his lips settled on hers.

It was cataclysmic—this unexpected, uncontrollable upheaval of her senses. What surprised her most was that such a gentle kiss could cause such an overwhelming rush of sensations. It was tender and poignant, and piercingly sweet. It was the way all first kisses should be: innocent, but with the promise of fuller pleasure to come.

Shawna felt her lips quiver in anticipation. She was afraid he was going to stop at that first touch, and it wasn't enough. She tightened her arms around his neck and pressed close against him. His arms tightened around her, till she felt the heat of his body begin to warm hers. Their lips melted in a deep kiss that added a touch of madness to the night.

His hand moved possessively over her back, with strong, sure, tantalizing strokes. And suddenly she knew there was a predatory tiger lurking inside that sweet man who had behaved with such perfect propriety all day. What had she unleashed with one simple encouraging hug? She felt a flicker of tongue stroke her lips, teasing them apart. He was holding her so tightly she couldn't get away if she wanted to...and she didn't want to.

One hand moved to her head, riffling her hair with strong fingers, while the other performed a spiraling massage on her back, intensifying as the circles diminished. And as he distracted her with these maneuvers, his tongue stole into the silken cavern of her mouth.

Hell must be like this, Shawna thought. Or was it only the loss of paradise? So much promise, and to know nothing could come of it. Because this man who kissed her as if his soul depended on it was a fraud. And a man who'd steal another man's work and put his name on it would ruthlessly steal a woman's heart, too.

She made a vain effort to escape. With her hands on his shoulders, she pushed him away. The moonlight gleaming in his eyes silvered them with menace, but his dreamy smile looked innocent.

"Just one more, for the road," he coaxed, and pulled her into his arms to kiss her again.

His plundering kiss made her legs weaken until, breathlessly, she broke away. He peered up uncertainly. "It's a long road," he said, his playful smile warning her he wasn't finished yet.

"No!"

As he reached for her, Shawna pushed him away. His precarious balance on the verandah railing sent him tilting backward. One hand instinctively grasped at her for safety. His legs entwined around hers, and for a moment they swayed outward on the railing. Her feet were off the round, her weight was on his chest, and she was sure they were both going to tumble to the ground below. But in that fraction of a moment that they hung suspended, she was acutely aware of the pleasure and excitement this close body contact caused. It wasn't just fear of falling that made her blood rush to her head and her heart pound so violently.

Why didn't they fall? Kurt had to be holding on to the railing for dear life. She slid backward off him in a body caress till her feet hit the floor.

"That'll teach me!" He laughed and helped her stand upright. "When you say no, you really mean it."

"I'm sorry. It's just that . . ." Shawna heard a small voice in her head finish the sentence. *Just that I'm falling in love with you, and that can't happen.*

"It's my fault. I got carried away. Must be the freckles," he said, and stood gazing at her with a somewhat fatuous smile pulling at his lips.

Kurt admired the fact that she was a little shy. He'd liked it when she tightened her arms around him earlier, too. He didn't want a cold woman, but a small town girl who wasn't too free with her kisses suited him fine. He was a patient man; he could wait for this one.

"Oh, I forgot to bring my sketch home," she exclaimed.

"You can get it tomorrow."

"All right. Thanks."

She looked at the door. It was time to go, before they started kissing again. . .such temptation. "See you tomorrow," she said.

Kurt gazed at her steadily, with a gentle smile on his savage face. "I can hardly wait," he said softly. "Good night, Shawna."

She watched him jog along the beach, back to his cottage, before going inside. Closing the door behind her, Shawna leaned against it and drew a deep sigh. What a night! She hadn't planned on anything like this when she'd volunteered to do a little investigating for Everett.

It seemed a lifetime ago that she'd first discussed this plan with Everett. It all seemed so simple then. But that was before she had actually met Kurt. She realized now that exposing him was going to hurt her as much as it hurt him. How had such a nice guy sunk to such depths?

The sooner she could get into his cabinets and see if he'd kept Everett's sketches, the better. Maybe tomorrow. And if not tomorrow, he'd mentioned having to be away for a few days on business. That would be the time to do it. *If* he went away, that is. He'd implied that he might delay the trip, because of her.

He had even invited her mother to visit him. That didn't seem like some jackal on the make. "Oh, damn Kurt Slater, anyway," she moaned and went up to bed.

Chapter Four

I'm glad to see you're dressed for the cool morning weather," Kurt said, when he called on Shawna at seven the next morning. He wore a brilliant smile, despite the early hour.

She was waiting for him, dressed in jeans and a fleecy, hooded sweater. Shawna hadn't had her coffee yet, and thus had to force a cheerful mood.

"I'm raring to go," she replied, with little enthusiasm.

"It can be pretty chilly just after dawn. Of course, you've spent time at the beach before."

To her dismay Shawna found that Kurt Slater looked just as attractive in the bright light of day as he had last night over their romantic candlelight dinner. His extravagant good looks didn't need any artificial aids. It wasn't just his eyes that were like the sea. *He* was like the sea—ever-changing on the surface, but below the surface there were undiscovered depths and mysteries. There had to be, because no one would ever guess to look at him that he was a thief.

"Do you want a cup of coffee before we go?" she asked. "Something warm inside feels good."

"I've already had one, but I'll join you in another, if you're fast."

"What's the rush?" she asked, as she poured two steaming mugs.

"Nellie doesn't like waiting."

"Don't tell me you've got another dog!"

Kurt accepted the coffee. "I'm a one-dog man. Nellie's my buggy. She's a pretty little thing—neat lines, loves the beach—but she's a bit temperamental. Maybe I should have called her Shawna," he added, lifting one of his mobile brows in a teasing smile that removed the last trace of Shawna's early morning grouchiness.

"I'm not temperamental!" she objected.

"Right, you're not temperamental, you're just a bad loser. I still haven't forgotten your fit of pique at Lighthouse Point yesterday. I bet you'll be practicing your tail off on that Windsurfer this morning while I slave over my hot drawing board."

It was exactly the way she planned to spend part of her morning. "I wouldn't mind learning how you executed that quick turning maneuver at the rock yesterday, without even slowing down."

"That's for experts. You shouldn't try it on your own. You'd smash either the board or your legs. And I wouldn't want you to wreck the surfboard," he said, but his warm smile belied the callous words. "You'll have to wait till later if you want an expert's help learning that stunt.''

Shawna tossed her head. ''Oh, is there an expert at Wells Beach?'' she asked impishly.

''No, at Slater's Beach.''

''I won't need any help. I'm a self-starter,'' she boasted.

''It's the finish at the rock that's hazardous. I'll be keeping an eye on you from my window. If you get stranded, just wave your bathing suit and I'll come to your rescue.''

''My bathing suit? Dream on.'' Shawna tossed her head saucily. ''Besides, I won't be floundering on the rocks.''

''Famous last words.''

They drank their coffee quickly and went out into the cool morning air. A layer of mist hovered over the sea and strayed inland, clinging to the ground. Through the haze, Shawna saw the shiny blue dune buggy, with Brix perched on the hood, waiting.

''You don't mind that we have company?'' Kurt asked. ''I don't want her getting too jealous.''

''This is the first time I've ever formed part of a triangle with a dog.''

''Who do you usually form triangles with?'' Kurt asked, glinting a wicked grin at her. ''I'd really like you two to get along. Brix doesn't make the whole trip. She usually bales out after the first lap. This is her hour for clam digging.''

''I'm the intruder. Sorry, Brix.'' Shawna patted the dog's head.

Brix yapped a welcome, and they settled into the vehicle. It was crowded with the dog, but as Kurt had forecast, Brix soon jumped out and went her own way. "Nellie" was a wild buggy. The drive was exhilarating. It was like being alone in the world. Not a soul stirred yet along the stretch of beach. Houses were scarce and far between.

They didn't talk much. It was enough just to feel the spindrift on their faces and the wind blowing through their hair. The ocean stretched off to the horizon on one side, and before them the beach was unmarked, except for the sand waves left behind by the tide.

At times he drove through a few inches of water; at others they sped over sand several yards inland. After a while he stopped where the ocean curved into a rocky bay.

Kurt gazed around at the scenery with an air of infinite satisfaction. "At this hour of the day, I feel the world is mine. That's why I like to come out early," he said.

"Is that what you'd like, Kurt? To own the whole world?"

He considered it before answering. "It's not a question of being acquisitive. I guess what I really mean is I'd like to have been here a few million years ago, when the world was like this, unspoiled and full of promise. No species was endangered yet, there were no oil spills, no acid rain, no such thing as money. Money can be a destroyer, too." Shawna listened closely, trying to fit all this into her profile of Kurt Slater. His mention of money made her perk up. "Money's a necessary evil," he added.

"It's the love of money that's the root of evil, not the money itself."

His jaws tightened, and his eyes clouded over as he looked out to sea. "Yeah, it's depressing what people have to do sometimes for money."

She felt they were skating on the edge of what he had done for money, and ventured to press him a little further. Shawna purposely used an indifferent tone. "Work, you mean?" she asked.

"That goes without saying. No, I didn't mean honest work. I meant the lamentable shortcuts people have to take sometimes."

"No one *has* to cheat, if that's what you're talking about." She listened, her heart pounding, to hear what he'd say.

His brow was furrowed, and when he answered, his voice was reluctant. "I think some people do. Something in their nature can't accept failure. Some people have such a compulsion to succeed, they'll do anything. I'm not just talking about monetary success, but all that goes with it, the life-style, the acclaim. Maybe we shouldn't be too hard on people like that. I suppose it's a sort of mental sickness."

Shawna's heart hardened. He was pretty easy on himself. "I think it's disgusting!" she exclaimed angrily.

Kurt just nodded, with a lazy smile tugging at his lips. "Good. The young should be idealistic. I expect you'll feel differently when you're older."

She stared mutinously. "I'm not that young, and you're not that old."

"Aging isn't just a matter of time. Our experiences have something to do with it, too. Shall we walk?"

It was an invitation to drop the subject. As they walked along, Shawna kept enough space between them so that Kurt couldn't take her hand. She didn't want him to touch her. His words had sounded like a betrayal. He was using his impoverished youth as an excuse to cheat. But poverty didn't always breed greed and overriding ambition, and she wouldn't let him excuse himself so facilely.

"I'm afraid I disagree with you about this cheating thing, Kurt," she said in a harsh voice. "You excuse people too easily."

He shook his head and gave a rueful smile. "Let's not talk about it now. This place is too beautiful to spoil with reality. Look at those rocks!"

Before them a tumble of enormous rocks looked as if they'd been dumped into the bay by a giant's dump truck. Each one would weigh tons, yet they were discrete rocks, not mountains.

"Imagine the turmoil of nature that caused that formation," he said, in a voice filled with awe. Then he reached down and picked up a handful of dry sand. "And then there's this," he added, as it sifted through his fingers. "Made by the same intelligence. It defies human understanding. 'To see the world in a grain of sand.'"

She gave him a skeptical look. "You're quite a philosopher."

"William Blake was the philosopher who hit on that happy phrase. I like to come here. It makes me realize how short life is, and how important it is to squeeze twenty-four hours out of each day. These rocks and even these grains of sand will still be around when we're long gone. What we do isn't that important."

"As long as we do it honestly," she added.

Kurt studied her, a serious, searching, satisfied look. "I thought you'd feel that way. I'm going to feed you now, and see if I can get you into a better mood. Do you want to drive to the restaurant?"

"Restaurant? I thought—"

"You thought I was going to cook? I usually stop off in Wells Beach when I drive in the morning. They make great waffles."

The morning outing had sharpened her appetite. Shawna had driven a dune buggy before and enjoyed being at the wheel. It took more attention than driving a regular car on a paved road, and occupied her mind. Kurt directed her to the restaurant, which was actually a truck-stop diner. When he called the proprietor by name, Shawna guessed that he came here fairly often.

The truck-stop served the best waffles and bacon she'd ever tasted, or maybe it was her sharp hunger that made her think so. The waffles were golden and crisp, smothered in maple syrup. They didn't talk much over breakfast, which gave her time to think. The more she saw Kurt Slater, the less she felt she knew him. He was an enigma. Fame and money seemed very important to him, yet he ran away from it all and hid himself in an isolated cottage by the sea.

Kurt Slater, a man who could hire a cook or dine in the finest restaurants, chose to eat in a truck-stop. He didn't even seem to have much interest in clothes. His cotton shirt was well faded, and she'd noticed that the hems of his jeans were ragged. Of course, he had that other life in New York. This was just a break for him, a change of pace. She knew that in New York he frequented gourmet restaurants and wore elegant clothing. He dated beautiful women there, too, yet he seemed to like her.

Was she just another change of pace? A little relaxation from the beautiful and sophisticated women he usually went out with? That must be it. She was waffles and coffee; they were caviar and champagne. And when he'd had his fill of rusticity, he'd dash back to his life in the fast lane.

The proprietor came over to their table when they finished eating, and Kurt introduced him. "This is an old friend, Ed Brown, Shawna."

"Pleased to meet you, Shawna. Would you folks like some more coffee? The second cup's on the house."

"Thanks, fill 'em up, Ed," Kurt said.

"Have you heard from your folks lately?" Ed asked.

"I was talking to them last week. It was nearly a hundred degrees in Arizona. They were wishing they were back home in God's country."

Ed laughed. "They won't feel that way come December. Are you coming out for practice tomorrow night?"

"I may have to go to the city, but I'll be here for the game." He turned to Shawna and explained. "Baseball. I'm pitcher for the Wells Beach team."

"Keep that arm exercised," Ed advised.

"I will. Tell Sally the waffles were great, as usual."

Ed left to wait on other customers, and Kurt explained that Sally was Ed's wife. "We all went to school together. Half our old school team still meets to play ball once a week. I like keeping in touch."

More rusticity. "Roots are important," she said.

"You don't talk about yours much, Shawna."

It was an invitation to open up about her life. Shawna had told so many lies that she didn't want to get into that dangerous area of reality. "I guess I just take all that for granted. I see my old school friends regularly, the ones who are still in town."

"It's like water. You never miss the water till the well runs dry, and you don't miss your old friends till you've lost them."

"You won't have that problem."

"Oh, I did! I guess I haven't mentioned I lived in the city for a while. I had a bit of success and it went straight to my head. Coming from a little dot on the map like this, I was overwhelmed by the Big Apple." He frowned.

This was the first time he'd mentioned living in New York, and Shawna listened intently. "New York, huh? When was that, Kurt?"

"A few years ago. I made a jackass of myself, started running with a fast crowd, didn't come home to visit except for Christmas. I acted like a real jerk, so I have some fence-mending to do now. That's why I make a point of coming here, to Ed's place, and playing ball with the guys."

Shawna was more interested in his city life. "The wine, women and song route, was it?" she prodded.

"Not in that order, but you have the ingredients right. It was a dead end, a waste of time. When I realized my work was going downhill, I moved back home. Luckily I can do most of my work here, but I have to go to New York once a week or so."

"You mentioned to Ed something about leaving tomorrow."

"I hoped I could put it off till after you left, but something came up. I have some work I have to do this afternoon in preparation for the visit, but I hope I can see you tonight."

"I'm feeding you, remember?"

A smile glowed in the depths of his stormy eyes. It had a peculiar warming effect on Shawna. "Would I forget that?" he asked softly. "I really should be getting home now. Will you be able to entertain yourself all day?"

"Hey, I didn't expect to find a recreation director next door when I came down here, you know. Of course I can entertain myself. I have to figure out how you executed that neat turn at the lighthouse rock. That should take nearly half an hour," she added, with a jeering look.

"Lady, that'll occupy your whole day. Just don't forget about my dinner."

By the time they drove home the mist along the shore had burned away. The air was warmer, and Shawna did intend to get out the Windsurfer, just as soon as she called Everett and checked in.

Kurt was coming for dinner at seven, which left her nearly eleven hours to kill. As it was still too early to call Everett, she wandered out to the porch and gazed at the ocean. The moisture-laden air carried its own inimitable scent. After this week, the ocean would always remind her of Kurt Slater. She felt an ache of lonesomeness that he'd be leaving tomorrow, and she'd probably never see him again. Not on intimate terms at least. They might meet at some business functions in New York, but that would be only an embarrassment.

While he was away, she meant to search his house and find the evidence to stop him from further piracy. Once she'd done that, she'd prefer not to see him again—ever. It would be too painful.

Shawna thought she understood why he'd stolen Everett's designs. Slater's career had gotten off to a flying start, but after his carousing period, his work had begun to slip. So he took the easy way out: he stole the best designs around, and adapted them enough to pass them off as his own.

But apparently he'd reformed . . . so why had Everett's spring designs been stolen? Maybe someone else had taken them. A persistent seed of hope began to swell. Maybe it wasn't Kurt this time. He had used Nancy Alton to help him, and Nancy no longer worked for Everett. On the other hand, it seemed unlikely that two different designers would pick Everett as their prey. It had to be Kurt. After all, Everett's designs had won him the award, and that would be a strong inducement.

Her fierce hope was that Kurt had reformed, but she owed it to Uncle Max to do what she could to help. Revenge didn't seem very important now. She just wanted Kurt to stop. He was talented. If he wasn't a good designer, he could be a commercial illustrator. The sketch he'd done of her last night was stunning.

Shortly after nine o'clock, Shawna called Everett's office. "Any luck yet?" he asked eagerly.

"Not so far, but he's leaving tomorrow. That's when I'll get in and search."

"Be careful now, Shawna."

"He'll be in New York. It'll be all right, don't worry. I was just thinking, Everett, about those designs that are missing now. Do you think someone else might have taken them? I mean, Nancy isn't working for you, and how could Kurt have gotten into your office?"

"She could have had my keys copied before she gave them back."

"Didn't you have the locks changed?"

"I asked her for the keys back. I'm afraid I didn't bother changing the locks. I'm too trusting."

"Slater isn't seeing Nancy now though, is he?"

"*Au contraire*, my dear. They're a hot item. I hear around town that she's working for him. She started a week before my office was rifled. Draw your own conclusions."

Hope dimmed. Suddenly, her voice seemed to elude her but she had to say something. "I see. Well, that's about all the news here. How's everything in New York?"

"About the same as usual. Keep in touch."

"I will. Bye."

When Shawna hung up the phone, she felt as though she'd aged a hundred years. Disappointed and listless, she dreaded the day that stretched before her. She dreaded dinner, too. Time would drag on interminably if she didn't do something. She might as well get out the Windsurfer and try to learn Kurt's trick. She decided to try it away from the rocks first, to avoid an accident. There was no reason why she couldn't practice it in front of Spindrift Cottage. If she mastered the stunt, she'd go over to the rocks.

It felt good to work her muscles. Learning the fast turn preoccupied her mind, easing away nervous tension. It looked so effortless when Kurt did it, but there was a lot of skill involved in knowing exactly when, and how much, to alter the set of the sail. She had to brace her whole body, especially her legs, for the sudden jerk. She took several splashes in the icy sea before she began to get the knack of it. Still she was reluctant to try it at Lighthouse Point.

Exhausted and cold, she returned home for lunch. Her gaze turned wistfully toward Kurt's cottage. They might as well have lunch together.... But she didn't want to force herself on him. What she really wanted was for him to confess, and tell her he had reformed.

She could forgive one fall from grace. Nobody was perfect. Yet except for that one fault, Kurt was about as close to perfect as she'd ever encountered. Wanting something hot to warm her shivering body, she opened a can of soup. She ate it alone, with the radio and a fashion magazine for company. After she had eaten, she turned again to the article on the new designers, and sat gazing at Kurt's picture.

It was a good, professional photograph, but his charm couldn't be captured in a still shot. He was volatile—ever-changing. It was evident in the way he carried himself, the way his eyes changed from clear to stormy, the way he smiled...the way he touched her.

When Shawna realized she was mooning over the picture like a teenage girl over a movie star, she turned to another article, looking to see if Everett was mentioned. This piece focused on the older, established designers. The other top designers were mentioned, but Everett's name was conspicuously absent. There was no article on him. That would really hurt his pride.

She read the article through and found his name in an aside in the second to last paragraph.

The old-style formality of the days of Everett are gone forever, like the hats of Lily Daché. The few designers of that old school who survive either design for aging European royalty or design derivative styles, aping the younger school, with indifferent success. To paraphrase Tennyson, "The old order changeth, yielding place to new, and fashion fulfills itself in many ways."

She closed the magazine with a scowl. "Aping the younger school," was it? One member of the younger school had won himself an award by aping Everett. She felt as hurt as if the article had personally attacked her. Everett was like family to her. Her mother had often told her about the glory days, when Everett was king, and she was his princess. Her face and his creations were on the cover of all the major magazines. Not just fashion magazines, either.

Of course, that was a long time ago, and the world of fashion moved swiftly. None of the other students in her class were breaking down Everett's doors to work for him. She probably wouldn't have gone there herself if it weren't for the special relationship between them. He hadn't been as receptive to her ideas as she'd hoped, but she was still learning a lot from him.

School didn't teach a designer the insider's tricks of knowing where to go for the best material at the best price. Everett's name was still big enough that the stores were always willing to check him out. Everett knew what suppliers were reliable, and the man had a fantastic eye for quality. He was a little conservative about mixing materials and trim, but she could experiment in that area when she was on her own.

At one o'clock, she set the magazine aside and began to think about dinner. She remembered the stand at Wells Beach that sold fresh seafood. Kurt had served lobster. She wanted to make him something different and decided upon clams. Not the hard shell quahogs; the littlenecks and cherrystones were usually eaten raw, and she didn't like that. The bigger ones were only good for chowder. She would shop for the soft clams that were delicious whether steamed or fried or served in chowder.

And driving into Wells Beach would be a diversion. She made a ritual of shopping, selecting the freshest clams and choosing things to go with them. A stick of crusty French bread, fresh salad fixings, and, of course, dessert. The heady aroma from the bakeshop lured her inside. After agonizing over the various temptations, she settled on a cherry cheesecake.

Shawna drove home and began preparing dinner. The salad had to be made, the clams for frying had to be pulled out of the shells, the batter prepared. She'd bought so many that she decided to steam some, in case Kurt preferred them that way. She put the white wine in the refrigerator to chill and arranged the table nicely. The cottage didn't provide fine accoutrements, but she found a red-and-white-checked cloth, and counted on the dimness of candlelight to hide the cheap crockery.

When everything but the last-minute cooking was done, she went upstairs and took a long soak in the tub. With flower-scented bubbles foaming under her chin, she sat, thinking, till the water grew cool. A deep sadness overcame her, and she found herself thinking of her mother.

Mom would like Kurt, and she realized Kurt would like her mother, too. They were similar in many ways. Mom had told her that Adele—she called herself Adele when she wanted to disassociate herself from that part of her past—had had a rather wild period. New York and fame went to her head. And when she met Dad, she'd latched on to him for dear life.

For a few years Adele continued commuting to New York to model, but it became just a job then, a way to make money. She wanted the money to buy the house in Connecticut that had become her refuge, and eventually became the family home. Like Kurt's cottage. Yes, they would get along just fine.

When the water grew cool, Shawna got out. Since her mother was still on her mind, she decided to phone her.

"Everett told you what I'm doing here?" Shawna asked. She hadn't told her mother earlier, for fear she'd forbid it. Mothers tended to think you were a child forever.

"He did, and I want you to know, Shawna, I disapprove. Let Everett do his own dirty work. He was always a user."

Shawna gaped in shock. "Mom! I never heard you say anything like that before! I thought you liked Everett."

"Oh, I do like him, but this is going too far. You'll be arrested for breaking and entering. And this is really none of your business, Shawna."

"Everett told you about..." The words stuck in her throat. She didn't want to call Kurt a thief.

"Everett was always paranoid about his designs. Seldom a year passed when he didn't think someone was stealing his ideas, whether he ever had them down on paper or not."

"But he *did* have these ideas down on paper, Mom, and they were taken."

"A lot of that goes on in the industry, dear."

That didn't make it right. "What did you mean, Everett's a user, Mom?"

"He chews people up and spits them out. You know he fired Nancy Alton last year for no earthly reason. And she wasn't the first."

There had been a very good reason for firing Nancy, and as far as Shawna was concerned, not revealing it showed kindness on Everett's part. "There may be more to that than he told you," she said vaguely. "Who else did he fire?"

"Dozens of models. Whenever a dress didn't sell, he blamed the model."

"Well, I must say, I'm surprised to hear you complain about him, after all these years. You always talked as though he were a king."

"That's because I used to work for him. He likes to be treated that way—you must have noticed. It just became a habit."

"Naturally, he expects to be treated with respect. You seemed to think it was a good idea for me to go to work for him."

"I knew he could teach you a lot. He still enjoys a solid reputation in the business. It will be a good training ground for you, but that doesn't mean you should let him involve you in anything underhanded like this. I really wish you'd leave, Shawna."

"He didn't ask me to come. He didn't even want me to. It was my own idea, Mom."

"Then he won't mind if you leave," her mother said reasonably.

"Well, I will be leaving soon. Maybe tomorrow."

"Good. You and I must have a long, serious talk about Uncle Max when you get home."

The call left Shawna feeling even worse than before. She had never sensed anything but approval from her mother, where Everett was concerned. He was always polite to her and thoughtful of his employees. Of course, she'd only been with him for a few months, and her relationship with him was rather special. The others wouldn't complain to her if they were unhappy with Everett. As she thought about it, she realized that his staff did change rather quickly. Two employees had left since she'd started work in May.

And while he was kind to her, he was really not very helpful with her design work. She was learning the mechanics of her trade, but design was the heart and soul of it, and she hadn't made any progress in that area. She had expected criticism from a master of the craft, but Everett's comments were neither constructive nor helpful.

Her mother probably knew Max Everett better than anyone else, and if Mom thought he was paranoid, it was possible Everett had just imagined that Kurt ripped off his designs. There had been striking similarities, but striking differences, too. Fashion went in waves. It often happened that two top designers showed similar designs.

It was one more slim ray of hope to cling to, and Shawna clung for dear life. She still planned to check out Kurt's house tomorrow when he was gone; she owed Everett that much. But now she hoped she wouldn't find anything incriminating.

The matter filled her mind as she dressed for the evening. She had carefully left all her Everett originals at home, and brought with her only casual clothes. Of these, she chose the fanciest, a green flowered wraparound silk jersey skirt that came to her ankles, and a white eyelet vest, buttoned in a low V at the front. This time, she remembered her earrings.

The morning sun had left a ruddy glow on her skin, which helped conceal her freckles. She brushed her hair, smoothed on a touch of lip gloss, and was ready to entertain Kurt Slater, designer extraordinaire.

Chapter Five

Kurt arrived at Spindrift Cottage at seven sharp. Along with the sketch of Shawna, he brought a bottle of champagne. "Special occasions should be celebrated," he said, as he handed the bottle to her. His smile held the promise of a very special evening.

There was a hint of the city Slater in his appearance tonight. Kurt looked elegant in a light sport jacket and fawn-colored trousers. His linen shirt, open at the neck, showed enough tan chest to stir vivid memories. The formality of a jacket was lightened by a pair of well-worn shoes.

Shawna took only a passing glimpse at his clothes. Her attention was riveted by his smile, and the hungry way he looked at her. He seemed to savor her presence, as if he'd been waiting all day for this minute, and now that it had arrived, he meant to enjoy it to the fullest. She reminded herself of his philosophy about enjoying every minute. His piercing gaze certainly made this moment intense. And the charged air told her that it was going to be a special evening for them.

Shawna took her portrait from him and examined it again. It was even better than she remembered. She knew she would always treasure it, no matter what happened between her and Kurt.

"The champagne's been chilled," he told her. "We should either open it, or put it on ice."

"Let's open it." Shawna had placed wineglasses on the table. Kurt popped the cork. They both laughed when it ricocheted off the wall, nearly knocking over a lamp on the rebound.

"Let's make a toast," she suggested.

The popping cork and the fizz of champagne lent a festive note to the party. Shawna's spirits rose with the bubbles. For tonight she would forget her troubles and enjoy an effervescent evening. Kurt stood, staring at her, with that intense, anticipatory hunger in his eyes.

Kurt already felt giddy, and he hadn't even poured the wine yet. It was Shawna that had turned this ordinary summer into a special, golden time. Ever since her arrival, he'd felt this heady excitement, like his first showing. It was the moment of anticipation that was so intoxicating, the uncertainty....

Many women more beautiful than she had thrown themselves at him. They were available to a successful designer, whether they were married or not. But he felt in his bones that his fame wouldn't influence her. If she liked him at all, she liked him for himself. That was important to him. And right now her shining eyes told him that she was definitely attracted to him.

What was it about her that had awakened all his old ideals? She wasn't even beautiful. She was cute, innocent and even a little saucy. She had a competitive streak a mile wide, and she would certainly voice her own opinions. She was an idealist, a woman with a hopeful view of the world. A man needed an idealist to inspire him to give his best.

He had almost given up on finding someone like her, a woman who wasn't merely smitten by his celebrity status. But sooner or later he would have to tell her the truth. If there was to be anything lasting between them, she would soon realize that he wasn't a struggling illustrator. Would it affect the way she felt about him? She would undoubtedly resent his little deceit. He'd have to be careful about how he explained that.

"You propose the toast," Shawna said.

He lifted his glass and touched hers. Their eyes met over the rims and held. "To the start of a beautiful friendship," Kurt proposed.

Shawna felt a lurching sensation in her chest. It was hard to drink to friendship when her every action was a betrayal. "Let's just drink to..." But she couldn't think of anything.

"To us? I like that," he said, and drank.

Shawna lifted her glass. The bubbles burst against her nose and tingled in her throat. She drank quickly, to dissipate the sad mood that was building in her.

"What do you have against friendship?" Kurt asked.

"Nothing! It just seems..."

"Not quite the right word?" he suggested. "I hope that we can be more than friends one day, Shawna."

"Yes," she said in a small voice, holding her glass out for a refill. "Where's Brix tonight?" she asked, hoping to change the subject.

"Tied up in the back of the yard. I was afraid she'd unmake my bed if I left her inside. She knew I was coming to see you."

"How'd she know that?" she asked, sitting on the sofa and inviting Kurt to join her.

"She figured it out. She knows when I put on a shirt and jacket that I'm going to see a lady, and that always sets her off."

"She's possessive, huh?"

Kurt studied her intently until she began to feel nervous. "I don't mind that. It's flattering really. I'm possessive myself, to a point."

"It's a sign of insecurity," Shawna replied.

"Yes, like jealousy. Did you ever know two people who really cared about each other who weren't at least a little jealous?"

Shawna thought of her mother and father. Dad had always been a little jealous of Everett, she thought. "No, I guess not."

"But why are we talking about jealousy?" He inclined his head closer and smiled a devastating smile that warmed her deep inside, like a heady sip of brandy. Lamplight burnished his chestnut hair to copper, and highlighted the sheen on his rugged features. "You haven't been fooling around with some other guy behind my back, have you? You don't have to answer that. Brix and I kept a pretty close watch on you. Too bad you didn't master the rapid turn trick. I'll teach you when I get back from New York."

"So you're definitely going?" She was almost relieved. These dinners were becoming too close for comfort.

"I couldn't get out of it. I wonder if you'd mind doing me a little favor while I'm away?"

"Of course." She smiled encouragingly.

"Brix," he explained. "She doesn't know how to behave in the city. I've tried, God knows I've tried."

"Naturally you couldn't leave her in a hotel room all day while you work, and you can't take her on your business errands." Shawna spoke calmly. She knew Kurt had some sort of home in New York, but his deceptions were easier to deal with than her own. His white lies were almost welcome, as reminders that this attractive man wasn't what he seemed.

"Actually I have an apartment there, but Brix would still be alone. She can't get the sheets off the water bed. I hate to think what chaos she'd cause in frustration. Probably gnaw a hole in the mattress and flood the whole apartment."

So he was admitting now that he lived in New York! That was interesting. Shawna made the proper exclamation of surprise. "An apartment in New York! Lucky you! It must cost a fortune."

"It wasn't cheap, but real estate in New York is a sound investment."

"You actually own it? Illustrating must pay well."

Kurt's nervous movements betrayed his guilt. "As I said, I'm becoming established in my career. About that favor—"

"I'd be happy to mind Brix. Just bring her over before you leave."

"The thing is, she prefers to be at home. She'll howl like a banshee if she's kept here. You wouldn't get any sleep. I was hoping you could go over and feed and water her, and let her run on the beach a little. I'll leave you the key, and I can show you where I keep her food."

"Oh, I see. That's fine." A curl of fevered excitement tightened in her chest. This certainly made searching his house easy! But her feelings of betrayal were compounded because he trusted her.

Noticing her reluctance, Kurt amended, "If you'd rather not, I can take her over to Ed and Sally Brown. They've watched Brix for me before."

"No! No, I'd be happy to do it, really."

He gave her a teasing smile. "It's all a clever trick on my part to make you and Brix get along."

"Getting along" didn't matter for a friendship of a few more days. Kurt was still thinking in terms of seeing her after her vacation, and she didn't know whether that made her feel pleased or frightened. At the moment, he was studying her with growing interest. She decided to escape before anything happened.

"I'd better start dinner. You have another glass of champagne. I won't be long."

"You can't drink champagne alone. It's against the rules. I'll help in the kitchen. What are we having?"

"Clams. I got some in Wells Beach this afternoon."

"Great! Quahogs or soft?"

"Soft—steamed and fried. Which do you prefer?"

"I love them all ways, raw, steamed, breaded, but best of all in a clambake. We'll have to have an old-fashioned clambake before you leave, Shawna. Let's

make it a firm date for this Friday night. I'll be back
by then. I'd like you to meet my friends.''

An old-fashioned clambake on the beach sounded
like fun. She would like to meet Kurt's friends. You
could tell a lot about a man by his friends, and how
they acted together. ''That sounds like fun,'' she
murmured. Shaking away a wisp of regret, she turned
her attention to dinner.

Kurt volunteered to steam one batch of clams while
she fried the other. Her batch was already shelled,
battered and ready to pop into the oil. While they
bubbled in the pan, Shawna got out the salad and
bread and lit the candles.

''You've gone to a lot of trouble,'' Kurt said, when
they sat down at the table. ''This looks charming.
Where did a landlubber learn to cook clams?''

''Haven't you ever heard of refrigeration? We get
fresh clams in Lewiston.''

''Day-old fresh,'' he said disdainfully. ''Have you
ever been to a clambake, Shawna?''

She hesitated a moment. They had often had them
at home, but she didn't want to sound too familiar
with beach life. ''No, it sounds like fun,'' she repeated in confusion.

''It is. Clambake is really a misnomer for the way we
do it here. It's a kettle clambake. First you line the
bottom of a kettle with washed seaweed. Then you line
the seaweed with fresh lobsters.''

''For a *clam*bake?''

''As I said, it's a misnomer. Next you line the lobster with green corn, still on the husk. Then you line
the green corn with a ton of clams still in the shell. You
add more seaweed on top, and boil the bejeebbers out

of it all. It usually takes an hour and a half or so before the clams are shucked. In the interval, you drink a lot of cold beer. Somebody plays a guitar, and you all sing. 'Goodnight Irene' and 'On Top of Old Smokey' are required selections. After that, you can ad lib. When the clams are done, you start at the top and eat your way through to the lobsters.''

She smiled at his enthusiasm. ''Then you call an ambulance and have the participants taken to the closest hospital.''

''No, then you sit and sing till you can move again. If anyone's had more beer than he should, he sometimes tackles the ocean. You haven't lived till you've attended an old-fashioned New England clambake.''

''What do you have for dessert?'' she asked. ''You haven't forgotten my lust for desserts?''

''Another bottle of beer, usually. But for you, we'll change the tradition. You can supply whatever you want.''

''We used to call a night like that a beer bash.''

''Ah ha!'' He laughed. ''I see you've had your dissipated moments, too. And here I thought I'd found a nice simple, small-town girl.''

She examined him closely. ''What would you want with a simple girl?''

''Simple in the sense of unspoiled. A nice girl is what I mean. I don't believe a beer bash or two have depraved you.''

Their conversation was lighthearted, but even in jest she could perceive the direction of his thoughts. As they talked on, she noticed his disenchantment with the glitz and glamour of the fashion world. Of course the word ''fashion'' wasn't used, but illustrators used models, too, and she got the idea that Kurt was looking for a more down-to-earth woman. He must have become tired of the whirling jet set. Someone like the imaginary small-town woman she'd created was what he wanted now.

If he knew she was the famous Adele's daughter, used to the very sort of life he despised, what would he think of her? If she'd been working for Everett a few years ago, she would have met Kurt during his wine, women and song phase. He'd have mistaken her for a sophisticated lady, because she attended loads of parties. But she was only an eager onlooker. By last spring, when she joined Everett, he'd forsaken that life-style.

When the clam bowls were empty, Kurt leaned back and sighed. "That was a gourmet feast, Shawna. I declare you an honorary member of the New England beach fraternity."

"We're not finished yet. I have dessert."

"I see I'll have to expand my menus. In future, dessert will be called for."

"And it better not be a bottle of beer!" she warned, ducking into the kitchen for the cheesecake.

She held her smile till she was alone. All of Kurt's conversations were future-oriented. He talked about things they would do together: the clambake, sailing, sight-seeing.... And it all sounded delightful. Was there any way she could straighten out this mess and make that future possible?

They both settled for a very small slice of cheesecake. "I'll have to eat all the rest myself tomorrow," she said, looking at the nearly full plate.

"I see the thought brings a smile of regret to your face. You can feed some of it to Brix, but not too much."

"Shall we have coffee on the porch?" she suggested.

"A good idea, and later, when the moon rises, we'll walk off some of this food—if you're still speaking to me."

She looked at him in alarm. What did he mean by that? "We have to talk," he said. "I've been misleading you about myself."

He took her hand and they went outside. The western horizon was painted crimson by the glow of the setting sun. It shone through the mist to color the clouds phosphorescent red. Sitting side by side on the porch swing, they stared at the glorious sunset. Shawna didn't want to disturb the peaceful moment, but curiosity goaded her.

"What horrible thing have you done, Kurt, that you think we won't be speaking?"

"It's not exactly that. I have a confession." He set down his cup and reached for her hand. She watched as he steeled himself for the revelation.

Her heart pounded. He was going to confess about stealing Everett's designs, and what should she say? She was so vastly relieved that her throat felt choked. Whatever he'd done, she could forgive him, as long as he promised not to do it again. She had her own confession, but that would come naturally after his. It would require a few minutes of embarrassing explanation, then their friendship could be rebuilt on a firmer foundation.

Shawna was feverish with nervousness. A febrile glitter sparkled in her eyes. She didn't notice that she had tightened her fingers to a crippling grip. "Go on," she said. "I'm ready." Her voice was husky with emotion.

Kurt saw the tension in her shoulders, and felt it in her hands. A doubt shadowed his eyes. "I haven't killed anyone," he said. "It's just a little prevarication on my part. I'm not an illustrator, Shawna. I'm a fashion designer, a well-known one, though you apparently don't recognize the name Slater."

She looked at him expectantly. "Yes," she said. Her anxiety mounted.

Kurt shrugged his shoulders. "That's it. End of confession. I don't even know why I didn't tell you in the first place. I guess my conceit led me to think you'd recognize the name, and perhaps be influenced by my reputation."

She shook her head in confusion. "What? I—I don't understand." Was that all he was going to say? Wasn't he going to come clean about the real crime?

"It's really very simple. I told you I'm an illustrator. Well, I'm not. I'm a fashion designer. That's all."

"But you were going to confess something. . . ."

Kurt leaned his head back against the pillows and laughed. He felt light with relief. His great confession didn't mean a thing to her. She'd never heard of him! That certainly put him in his place. He wasn't as famous as he'd thought.

His arm fell to Shawna's shoulder, and he inclined his head toward hers. "You can relax, sweetheart. You make me realize that I still have some descending to go before I come down to earth. I thought you would recognize my name when I told you I was Slater. In my own field, I'm—well, a celebrity I guess," he said modestly.

Shawna felt numb. He wasn't going to admit about stealing Everett's work after all. She had overestimated either his conscience or his bravery. She had to say something. "Oh, *that* Slater. Yes, of course I've heard of him—you. But why on earth did you lie about it?" Maybe she could still urge him to a full confession.

He shook his head. "I don't know. Call it stupidity. In my line of work, I deal with a lot of beautiful women. I don't mean models in particular. The fast lane is littered with hangers-on, along for the ride, as it were. Some of them are very ambitious. Some of them are even willing to pretend they like you for yourself, when it's only your life-style they want. I want to apologize, Shawna. It was an insult to even *think* you might be impressed by a reputation. I knew you weren't like that. Deep down I knew it, but I didn't want there to be even a possibility that my reputation was influencing your feelings. I think we can safely assume that our friendship isn't based on that."

"No, of course not."

"That's why I said I lived here. I only live here for part of the year, though I do consider it home. These are my preferred digs, but I have to spend a lot of time in New York. So occasionally I travel."

She gazed deeply into his eyes. "Was there anything else you wanted to confess?" she asked uncertainly.

"That's about it."

"You mentioned something last night about a period of wine, women and song. Your work was slipping, you said."

Kurt made a dismissing gesture. "Oh—that. Yes, I thought I was God's gift to the universe for a few months. My simple country boy's head was turned by the glamour. I don't claim to be a saint now, but I straightened out my priorities before I went completely to the dogs."

"And your work? You managed to keep it up?"

"It was really the work that brought me back to my senses. The winter show was only a short time away, and I realized I didn't have anything new to show. I was just living on the glory of last year's success. You're only as good as your last show. That's when I hightailed it out of town and came back here to straighten out my head."

"And for the show, you managed to design a successful new line?" she asked warily. Now was his chance. He could admit he "borrowed" a few ideas, say something to acknowledge, however obliquely, that he'd stolen Everett's designs.

"Yes. My designs were late—I just slipped under the wire, but I made it. In fact, I won the Golden Needle Award for that particular line."

"Oh. That—that's nice, Kurt. Congratulations."

Kurt assumed she didn't know how important the award was. He would have enjoyed hearing praise from her, but that wasn't the important thing. He'd confessed, and she didn't seem to mind that he'd prevaricated a little. What surprised him was that Shawna didn't rip up at him for the implied insult to herself. Why wasn't she berating him for thinking that she was superficial enough to be influenced by a reputation? But she wasn't angry at all. She just looked a little confused, and very sad.

"Are you disappointed with me?" he asked.

"Why should I be?"

Kurt hunched his shoulders. "Well, you've been truthful and straightforward with me. I was a little devious. I thought you'd dislike that. That's why I wanted to get it off my chest before I leave."

Shawna sat with her hands in her lap, gazing out at the water. As the sun set, the ocean dulled from crimson to slate. She gave Kurt a fleeting look when he reached for her fingers and squeezed them. She felt as though he was squeezing her heart—her hard, cold heart.

He lifted one hand to her chin, and turned her head toward him. "Forgive me?" he asked, in a soft, coaxing voice. The sea-green depths of his eyes were clouded with doubt and uncertainty. He looked almost boyish, like a kid caught eating candy in school. His fingers moved to caress her cheek.

Their engrossing touch fired her with yearning. Shawna shook her head ruefully. She lifted her hand and covered Kurt's, holding it against her cheek a moment. If only that was all she had to forgive, one little lie.

"That's all right, Kurt. It doesn't matter," she said with a wistful smile. But her voice revealed her sadness.

"You *are* disappointed in me."

"Don't be silly. I don't even understand why you bothered lying. I mean, illustrator or designer, it doesn't make much difference."

His hand slid to the nape of her neck and rested there, massaging the tense muscles. "It wasn't the career so much as the—the degree of success I've been lucky enough to achieve. How could I think for a minute that any of that would matter to you? You're one in a million, Shawna Cassidy. I'm not going to let you slip through my fingers. You and I are going to see a lot of each other."

Her jaws moved, but she couldn't speak over the lump in her throat. She wanted to throw herself into his arms and cry in frustration. He was saying all the right things, doing all the right things—if only he'd prefaced it with a confession. She couldn't go on like this. Shawna steeled her nerves to ask him point-blank. But she'd let him know she could forgive, whatever he'd done, she had to forgive him...because she loved him.

"Kurt," she said in a voice breathless with determination, "I want you to..." But she couldn't go on.

His head was slowly, irrevocably descending closer, and she stared at the glitter of his eyes, hypnotized. A flutter of lashes hid the hypnotic daze, then his lips touched hers, and it was too late to stop. She wanted him too much to fight it. Her only objection was one rueful sigh of regret, just as their lips joined.

His arms reached for her, pulled her against him, and tightened possessively. Her heart lurched at the engrossing intimacy of her soft breasts thrust against the warmth of his chest. The hiss of the rising tide sounded far away, but its soft moisture filled the air. Then the sound receded, and she heard only the pounding beat of her heart. Her awareness was limited to the circle of his arms, where a new kind of magic occurred.

His gentleness was disarming. He didn't attack, but lured her onward with tender, nibbling kisses at the corners of her mouth. How could such a gentle man be anything but good? She felt her lips tremble open, and couldn't control them. When the moist flicker of tongue invaded her mouth, she found herself basking in the sweet torment of his kiss. He probed deeper, penetrating with gliding strokes that caused a melting sensation deep inside her.

When his hand moved to the front of her shirt, she put hers on top to stop him. But when he pushed the shirt aside, she didn't know whether she was guiding him or delaying his progress. As his warm fingers cupped her breast, hers seemed to be encouraging, pressing more tightly. His thumb looked for her nipple, grazing it with rough gentleness till it responded. A stirring quiver at the vital core of her being alerted her to danger.

She eased her hand away, but as a tremor of desire shook her, she slid it under his shirt. His chest moved erratically, revealing the sexual tension that was growing. Her fingers clung to the damp warmth of his body, edging closer to that enticing patch of crisp hair. She wanted to feel it. Suddenly Kurt pulled back. She looked at him in alarm.

"We can get more comfortable than this," he said in a husky voice, scooping her onto his lap.

Sanity returned, and she exclaimed, "No!"

But she was already nestled in his lap, with his strong arms drawing her closer against him. "I'll be gone for a couple of days, sweetheart." The words were muffled against her lips. His coaxing voice was irresistible.

As far as Shawna was concerned he'd be gone forever, and she wasn't strong enough to resist one last kiss. She looped her arms around his neck and swallowed a tear of regret as his lips found hers. It was a poignant, bittersweet kiss, beginning with a tender touching. It soon escalated to fiery passion, as they tasted and touched each other with their lips and hands, in a feverish exploration.

Breathless and half-delirious with desire, Shawna felt herself slipping deeper into madness. A last kiss was one thing. But she'd never given herself to any man, and she had to resist the yearning to do it now. It would be tantamount to a one-night stand, because there was no future for her with Kurt.

His hands went to her hips, moving her against him. She pulled them away. "Let's have that walk now," she said.

Kurt looked at her as though she were mad. "Walk?" It was a howl of protest.

"Walk," she insisted, and jumped up while he was distracted. "You know, put one foot in front of the other, heel, toe, heel, toe." Her voice settled down to normal once she was away from him.

Kurt glowered, but rose. "This is cruel and unusual punishment, lady."

Hand in hand, they wandered down to the beach. "I'll walk you home," Shawna said. "One of us better behave like a gentleman."

He gave an apologetic grin. "You're right. I got carried away. It was the thought of not seeing you for forty-eight hours. Hey, I've got an idea! Why don't you come to new York with me?''

They stopped walking, and he looked at her eagerly. ''It's a terrific idea. You can stay at my place.'' He lifted his hand to wave her to silence before she could object. ''Alone. I'll stay with friends. I'll be busy for most of the day, but we can go out in the evening. Or if you like, you can tag along while I work. No, that'd be boring for you. You'd probably rather shop or do some sight-seeing.''

''I couldn't.''

''Why not? You're on vacation. And your recreational director won't be here.'' He waited, smiling at her expectantly.

''This is my chance to practice the Windsurfer.'' It sounded like a limp excuse, even to her.

''Boy, when you said you liked the ocean, you weren't kidding. I can't tempt you?''

''Oh, I'm tempted all right, but I don't think I should.''

Kurt nodded. ''I understand. It isn't done in Lewiston. That's all right. I don't want to turn your mother against me before I even meet her.''

They continued their walk. ''I'll call you tomorrow evening, just to make sure Brix is taking good care of you,'' Kurt said. ''You might as well stop in at my place now and I'll give you the key and show you where Brix's food is.''

''There, you see!'' she said. ''I couldn't go if I wanted to. I have to baby-sit Brix.''

He grinned. ''Brix would really tear the place apart if she knew I'd forgotten all about her.''

"For a full five minutes. I'm flattered. I beat out a dog!"

"It wasn't even close," he said, as he kissed the tip of her nose.

They went into Kurt's cottage and he got the key from the kitchen. Cans of dog food were in the lower cupboard. He showed her the bowl and leash. "Would you like me to leave you the keys to Nellie?" he asked.

"I have my car, thanks."

"Well, I guess that's about it then. Now that you've walked me home, I have to show you I can be a gentleman, too. I'll walk *you* home."

They were just going to the front door when the phone rang. "Who could be calling at this hour?" Kurt asked, as he lifted the receiver. "Where?" he asked. His tone was a bark, and his face was grim. "I'll be right there."

He turned to Shawna. "There's a fire at Ed's place. That darned oil he uses for the fries. I *told* him...I've got to go, Shawna. We have a volunteer fire department here. I'll call you."

He was already running toward the front door. "Yes, go on!" she said, hurrying after him. The door slammed behind them.

Shawna stood alone, feeling useless. It didn't occur to her till she was halfway back to her cottage that this would have been an ideal time to search his cottage. As she walked along the beach, Kurt's key ring weighed heavily in her pocket. That key had become a symbol to Shawna, an example of Kurt's trust in her, and her deception. With a deep breath, she continued down the beach, deciding not to search the cottage tonight.

Chapter Six

Shawna was glad she had the cleaning up to do to keep her hands busy. The fire at Ed and Sally's restaurant was another distraction. She was concerned for them, though the acquaintanceship was slight. They were a hard-working, young couple, and she hoped the fire wasn't bad enough to put them out of business.

Inevitably, her thoughts soon turned to Kurt. She had to admire how quickly he ran to the aid of his friends. That he was a volunteer fireman at all was a point in his favor. It showed a real concern for his neighbors. Was it only strangers, competitors, who were fair game?

He didn't act like a man who took advantage. He could have taken advantage of her mood tonight without too much trouble, but he'd backed off as soon as she had objected. Whatever character flaws he had, she didn't think they would permit him to take advantage of someone he liked. And he liked her very much. Maybe "love" wasn't too strong a word for the relationship that was growing between them.

He was leaving tomorrow, and maybe that was for the best. She shouldn't have let herself get so deeply involved with Kurt Slater. She'd come here, bristling with indignation, to discredit him. Too bad she couldn't have accomplished it without falling under the spell of his charm. It was so sweet, the way he had worried about his great "confession."

Was it possible Everett was mistaken about Kurt? Shawna could hardly believe he'd done what Everett accused him of. Time hung heavy after the dishes were done. Her mind kept harping on Kurt, and she decided to drive over to the truck-stop diner and see how things were going there. Maybe she could help. She would have offered to go with Kurt, but she'd probably only have been in the way. What did she know about fighting a fire? Nothing, and gawkers were a nuisance. She'd stay well in the background.

It was only a few miles to the diner. The worst of the fire was over when she arrived, but the reek of smoke hung heavy on the air. The fire truck was still there, water ran in rivulets from the house, and neighbors were milling around. She examined the men in their yellow fire-fighting suits till she picked out Kurt, talking to Ed and Sally. True to her resolution, Shawna hung back and observed.

The front of the building didn't show any damage. The fire must have occurred in the kitchen. With luck, they may have confined it there. When the excitement began to die down, Shawna decided she could join the crowd without being in anyone's way.

"Was there very much damage?" she asked a teenager, who sat on his bike, looking at the building.

"The kitchen's a write-off, and there's a lot of smoke damage to the house. But nobody was hurt. Ed got the kids out all right."

"That's good. I wonder what the family will do. How many children do they have?"

"Two boys, Joe and Josh. Everybody's offered to put them up till they can get the house aired out."

The men began moving back to the fire truck. Shawna waited, hoping for a chance to speak to Kurt. When he was alone, she ran over and tugged at his elbow.

He looked surprised and happy to see her. "Shawna, what are you doing here?"

"I came to see if I can do anything to help. Is everyone all right?"

"They're fine. This fire may have been a good thing, in the long run. Ed isn't careful enough about safety in his kitchen. We've warned him before, but sometimes it takes an accident before it sinks in. As a matter of fact, there is something you can do. The Browns are staying with me for tonight. You can meet them at my place and let them in, see if they need anything. You know your way around the house."

"I'll be happy to. Do you have enough room for them all? There are two spare bedrooms at Spindrift Cottage."

"I have plenty of room, thanks. I should be home soon. We just have to drive back to the station, check the equipment and get our cars. Will you still be there when I get back?'' he asked.

She sensed the eagerness in the question. "I'll wait till you come."

"Good."

He patted her arm and left.

Shawna drove home and went to Kurt's place to wait for the Browns. She could go in now and search those cabinets in his living room, but told herself the Browns might arrive any minute. It was a good enough excuse to delay what she realized she had to do eventually.

Half an hour later the Brown family arrived. Their rambunctious boys, four and five years old, were enjoying the excitement immensely.

She went to meet Ed and Sally. "I'm so sorry about the fire," she said. "I've got Kurt's key. I'm right next door, if there's anything I can do to help. If you need clothes or anything, Sally . . ."

"I threw a few things into a bag. Get the bag, Ed?" she called. Sally was a few years older than Shawna, but the same general type—slight of build, and with tawny red hair. Although her busy life didn't leave her much time to fuss over her appearance, she exuded a healthy, natural beauty. Dressed in jeans and a sweat-shirt with her face smudged from smoke, she looked tired and worried.

They all trooped into the cottage. "Why don't I make some coffee?" Shawna suggested. "I don't imagine you folks'll be getting much sleep tonight."

"I'll help," Sally offered. "Honey, will you take this pair up to bed?"

Ed corralled the boys upstairs and Sally joined Shawna in the kitchen. "Will you be able to reopen the restaurant soon?" Shawna asked.

"It'll take the better part of a month. We have to rebuild the entire kitchen." She shook her head. "I don't know where the money will come from."

"Weren't you insured?"

"Not enough to cover the cost of rebuilding and restocking. Oh well," Sally added resignedly, "we'll get by somehow. I can always go back to working at the fish-freezing factory. But it won't be the same as working at home, with Ed and the kids."

Shawna felt useless. She wanted to help, but she certainly couldn't finance any rebuilding. "I'm sure it'll work out somehow," she said.

"Just look at me!" Sally exclaimed. "I'm going to run upstairs and change before Kurt gets home. There are some men you don't want to see you looking like this," she added, with a cheerful laugh.

"I know what you mean."

Sally gave her an assessing look. "Is it serious between you and Kurt?"

"Good heavens, no! I'm just renting the cottage next door for a week."

Sally smiled impishly. "A week should be long enough, if you work fast," she said, then ran upstairs.

Shawna refused to think about anything "serious" involving Kurt. Instead, she arranged cups and saucers on the table and filled the sugar bowl. When Sally returned, wearing clean jeans and a floral print blouse, they all sat down to sip coffee.

Ed patted his wife's hand consolingly. "I really goofed up, didn't I? I forgot to turn off the switch under the oil. A good thing we had the fire extinguisher."

"You wouldn't even have had that if Kurt hadn't nagged you about getting it," Sally sniped.

"Don't kick a man when he's down, Sally. I've learned my lesson. Next time..."

"Yeah, if there *is* a next time. We've lost our restaurant, and we could have lost our sons, Ed!"

When the turmoil was over, Sally broke down and cried, while Ed apologized some more and patted her shoulder. Shawna felt totally out of place during this private moment and said quietly, "I'll run along now."

Kurt was just driving up when she slipped out the door. "Are they okay?" he asked.

"As well as they can be, given the circumstances. Sally says they weren't adequately insured."

Kurt rubbed his chin thoughtfully. "Thanks for coming, Shawna, and for helping out."

"I didn't do anything. I wish I could help."

"Hey, you helped. Don't underestimate moral support. I'll be in touch with you before I leave tomorrow. I'll be getting a later start than I planned on. It looks like you might not have to baby-sit Brix after all. The boys'll be more than happy to entertain her."

"Oh, maybe I better give you the key then."

"Keep it for now. I don't know how long Ed and Sally are staying. Besides, I kind of like to think you have free access to my house."

It was about the worst thing he could have said. Shawna felt a terrible qualm of treachery. "I'll see you in the morning then. Bye."

Kurt kissed her on the cheek, and watched to see that she got home safely.

After Shawna was alone at Spindrift Cottage, she took out Kurt's key and put it on the counter. The darn thing was burning a hole in her pocket! It would be hard to search his house with the Browns there, but she wasn't entirely sorry, either. It was becoming harder by the minute to go on with this project. She didn't want to see proof of Kurt's deception. As long as she wasn't sure, she could go on hoping.

It was nearly one o'clock when she went up to bed. She leaned against the windowsill, looking out at the shifting sea. It was calm tonight. The swells were gently rolling, with no white caps. But its awesome power was there, a veritable giant, hidden by the calm surface.

In spite of the coffee and her worries and the excitement of the fire, Shawna soon slept. She awoke in the morning to drizzling rain. A rainy day locked in a cottage was about the dreariest prospect she could imagine. Hours and hours of inactivity. She glanced at her watch and saw that it was a lot later than she thought. The overcast sky had fooled her. It was nearly ten o'clock.

She jumped out of bed and scrambled into jeans and a warm shirt. Why was her heart beating so erratically? There was no reason she should have been up early. Except that Kurt was leaving this morning, and she was afraid she'd missed him. He might have tapped quietly on the door and left without awakening her. She was wildly, foolishly saddened to think she might have missed this last chance to see him.

She planned to run over to his cottage as soon as she was dressed, using the excuse of visiting the Browns. She was just running a brush through her hair when there was a knock at the door. Her heart revved like an engine. Kurt! She bolted down the stairs two at a time and opened the door.

Under his raincoat Kurt wore a well-tailored suit with a smooth, crisp shirt. For a flashing instant, he seemed like a stranger, but not a total stranger. Now he looked like *the* Slater, the elegant man whose picture appeared in newspapers and magazines, often with a beautiful woman on his arm. His coat collar was turned up against the rain, and his eyes had darkened to slate, to match the stormy sea. In any attire, Kurt Slater looked ravishingly handsome.

Shawna felt a smile soften her face. "Hi," she said, in a light voice.

"Good morning."

"You got a bad day for your trip. Can you come in for a minute?"

"Just for a second," he said, stepping in. "Actually, I was hoping for rain," he added.

"Why?"

"Because I don't like to miss a nice day at the beach. Selfish of me. This way, I know you won't be outdoors, finding yourself another boyfriend."

A warm tingle suffused her body. It was the word "boyfriend" that caused it. Did Kurt consider her his "girlfriend" then? His caressing eyes confirmed it.

"Do you have time for some coffee?" she asked.

"Not really. I'm already leaving a few hours later than I intended to. I'll have to take the second flight from Portland. I just dashed over to say goodbye. Make that *au revoir*," he said, drawing her hands into his. "We'll definitely be seeing each other again—very soon."

Kurt pulled her into his arms and held her against him. His raincoat, sprinkled with rain, felt cold. She pushed it aside and wrapped her arms around his waist. Kurt pulled her head to his chest and stroked her hair. They stood silently for a moment, just enjoying the closeness. She felt his chin resting on the top of her head.

"I wish I didn't have to go," he said.

She looked up eagerly. "Do you really have to?" Kurt smiled at the hope shining in her eyes. She looked like a kid, with her hair defiantly dipping over the edge of her eye. He smoothed back the wayward tendril.

"I'm afraid so, but I'll be back soon. Sure you don't want to change your mind and come with me?"

The Browns would be at his cottage. She couldn't search it, so... But no, why complicate this affair any further? "I'll just sit home and pine. Maybe I can help Ed and Sally."

"I don't know how long they'll be staying. Ed planned to spend the morning cleaning up at the diner, but Sally was going to stay at the cottage and keep the kids out of his hair. She mentioned something about going down to Wells Beach later, to stay with her mother."

Then maybe she *would* be able to search his cottage. It made another reason not to give in to temptation and go with Kurt. "I'll drop over to visit her and Brix later this morning."

"I wouldn't be surprised if the weather clears up by this afternoon. Be careful if you decide to give yourself some wind surfing lessons. We wouldn't want you hurting yourself. I told Brix to look after you."

Kurt's voice was beginning to sound husky. She knew by the glow in his eyes that he was going to kiss her. Mesmerized, she lifted her lips for his kiss. It was just one fierce, strong, possessive kiss, then he gently backed away.

"If I don't get out of here, I won't make it to the city today. I sure wish I could stick you in my pocket and take you with me. This is going to be the shortest series of meetings I ever held." He took the tip of her chin between his finger and thumb. "When I get back, Shawna Cassidy..." Her breath caught in her lungs. "We'll make up for lost time," he promised.

A rakish smile lifted his lips. He gave her a kiss on the tip of her nose, and left. Shawna shook the stardust out of her eyes and came down to earth with a thump. When he came back, everything would be different. She would either have found some evidence and have her fears confirmed, or she would be back in limbo, wondering. You couldn't go on wondering and doubting forever. She'd have to ask him outright, and that would tell him her whole presence here was a lie. Either way, he would despise her.

Shawna busied herself making coffee, straightening up the cottage, killing time. It was going to be a long day, and she was saving the visit to Sally as her one outing. By eleven, she was beginning to feel like a prisoner. She dashed out into the rain and ran over to Kurt's cottage.

Sally was flitting around Kurt's kitchen preparing a picnic basket of food to take over to Ed.

"Hi, Shawna." She smiled. "Come on in and have a seat." Sally looked less frazzled today. After a shower and a good night's rest, she was apparently feeling more like herself. "I was going to call you. Would you mind driving me over to the restaurant? Ed's got the car, and I want to take this lunch over to him."

"I'd be happy to. Where are the kids?"

"They're in the shed, sitting in Kurt's dune buggy, pretending they're driving it." She grinned. "Ever since Kurt took them for a few drives, they adore Nellie."

"Did you get any sleep?" Shawna asked.

"I slept till ten o'clock. Ed and Kurt fed the kids breakfast for me. It was like a holiday. I was just talking to Ed on the phone. Everything's going to be all right," she said, and smiled contentedly.

"I'm glad to hear it. Was there not as much damage as you thought last night?"

"The kitchen's totaled, and the dining room's a shambles from the smoke. But it'll be fun fixing it all up, getting new curtains and redecorating."

Shawna blinked in surprise. "I guess you've spoken to the insurance people?"

"We had some coverage. Kurt's lending us the rest of the money to redo the place. Interest-free," she added. "He's such a nice guy, and a good friend. The only condition is that Ed follows all the fire and safety rules this time."

Shawna experienced again the swelling, blooming feeling inside. Praise of Kurt was like praise of herself. "That was nice of him."

"Everyone in the community has been so generous. I've had dozens of calls from friends and neighbors offering clothes and stuff. Our neighbors are organizing a benefit clambake, with the proceeds going to help us. Isn't that sweet?" she said, shaking her head. "And when we reopen, they'll all be at the diner, trying to help us by eating there a couple of times a week. Kurt comes over for breakfast just about every day."

Shawna smiled. "If the rest of your food is as good as your waffles, it won't be any hardship for them."

"You should try my clam chowder," Sally boasted. "But I guess you won't be around much longer. You said you're only here for a week, right?"

"That's right."

"Well, you'll just have to come back and visit again."

Sally began wrapping up the sandwiches. "Can you take me to the restaurant now? Ed's been working for hours. He'll be ravenously hungry."

"Sure, right after I check on Brix."

"I'll call the boys."

In five minutes, the group piled into Shawna's car for the short drive. The rain was petering out to a drizzle. Sally invited Shawna to join the family for lunch, and as she'd made a huge pile of sandwiches, Shawna accepted. They ate in the family's living room with the windows open. The smell of smoke was still strong, and Sally passed the noon hour by mentally redecorating the room.

By the time they finished eating, the rain had stopped. Weak sunlight was beginning to filter through the cloud cover.

"I'll be home about five," Ed said.

"I'm going upstairs to collect all the linen and towels," Sally said. "I'll wash them at Kurt's place this afternoon. Might as well get started on the cleanup."

It sounded as though the Browns were going to make Shawna's search impossible—for today at least. When they arrived at the cottage, Shawna offered to help Sally. It seemed the only charitable thing she could do was get Joe and Josh out of Sally's hair for an hour. She took Brix and the boys for a run along the beach, gathering interesting stones and chasing the waves in and out. After an hour, the boys wanted to get back to Nellie, Kurt's dune buggy.

Shawna didn't feel like practicing on the Windsurfer that afternoon. She didn't feel like doing anything. Time hung suspended till she could search Kurt's house. In this uncertain, waiting period, she felt drawn to Lighthouse Point. She walked along to the bay of rocks, and out to the end of the point. The ocean was in a volatile mood, with huge dark swells pounding the coast. The churning water was nearly black, with just a tint of dark green. Even the foam that trailed in the waves' wake was light green from seaweed. The spindrift was violent today, flinging its salty spray in Shawna's face, nearly soaking her clothes.

How powerful nature was! Those waves looked strong enough to wash away even the huge monolith she stood on. What would it be like, to be carried out into the middle of that roiling, tempestuous sea? The ocean was one of the last untamed resources. When it unleashed its fury, man trembled and succumbed.

Shawna shivered and hurried back to her cottage. It was only four o'clock, and she felt as if the day had lasted a week already. In a restless mood, she drove along the coast, down to Kennebunkport, where she stopped at an inn for lobster and beer, then drove home. The Browns were still at Kurt's cottage. When Shawna saw some neighbors going in to visit, she knew she wasn't needed. She went to a movie in Wells Beach, and returned home at nine-thirty. The lights were all on in Kurt's cottage.

She phoned Everett. He was out and she left a message on his machine. Half an hour later, the phone rang, and she looked at it unhappily. She didn't really want to talk to Everett, but had felt she should check in with him.

"Hello," she said.

"You sound kind of sad. Does that mean you're missing me?"

"Kurt!" The vague feelings of discontent that had dogged her all day vanished like mist in the sun.

"I called you a couple of times this afternoon and didn't get any answer. I was afraid you'd gone and broken your neck on that fool Windsurfer."

"Wishful thinking!" She laughed. "I just went for a drive." Her voice was filled with delight.

Kurt heard it, and his own voice grew sultry. "If you think that's what I'm wishing at this minute, you're about a million miles off the mark."

"What are you wishing, at this very minute?" she asked.

"I'm wishing you were here, or better yet, that I was there. I got you a present."

"What?"

"That'd be telling, but you can model it for me when I get home. Does that give you a hint?"

"A dress?" An original Slater! Her first jolt of pleasure soon turned to dismay. One of Everett's employees could hardly wear a gown designed by the competition. It brought home very graphically the anomalous position she was in.

"Half a dress, sort of."

"Which half?"

"The half they wear in topless bars. You'll have to wear something else with it—at least in public."

"It sounds indecent!"

"It is, but très chic. All the ladies'll be wearing them over their bathing suits next year. Oh, and there's a sun hat with a big brim that goes with it. Completely impractical. The wind'll carry it away the first time you stick your nose out the door. Speaking of wind, how's the weather up there?"

"Balmy. It was rough today, but it's nice now." Shawna smiled at her own words. It wasn't nice at all. It was rough and windy and cold, but when she heard Kurt's voice, her world had suddenly brightened.

"It's lonesome here," he said, in an insinuating tone. "I may find myself running back sooner than I planned. I really shouldn't, though, or I'll only have to come back that much sooner."

"What are you doing tonight?" Shawna asked. She felt a sting of jealousy that he might be going out. Parties started late in New York.

"I already told you. I'm sitting here alone, wishing I were with you."

A smile of satisfaction curved her lips. "You didn't ask about Brix."

"How is she?"

"Fine. I took her for a walk with the Brown boys. And by the way, Kurt, it was kind of you to help the Browns."

"The cottage would have been sitting empty."

"I mean about the money. Sally told me."

"It's just business, a loan. Ed'll repay it," he said, dismissing the subject.

But Ed wouldn't be paying interest, and he wouldn't be harassed for the repayment, either. Shawna had come to know Kurt well enough to realize that.

"Don't be so modest. It was kind."

"I won't argue." There was a teasing lilt in his voice. "If I can fool you into thinking I'm a philanthropist, it won't do my cause any harm."

"What cause is that?"

"I'll tell you as soon as I get home. You take care of yourself now, you hear?"

"You, too. Bye, Kurt."

Shawna hung up the phone gently. Whatever Kurt might have done in his wine, women and song period, she could content herself that he was basically a kind, generous person. It seemed less possible every day that he'd ever resorted to stealing. Why didn't she just tell Everett that she hadn't found anything, or that she couldn't get into the cottage? He hadn't wanted her to come in the first place.

But then she'd be cheating, too. If she were to go on seeing Kurt, she'd have to tell him sooner or later that she wasn't a secretary from Lewiston, but Maxwell Everett's friend and employee. And once he knew who she really was, his faith in her would be shattered.

Shawna didn't call Everett again, and he didn't return her call. She assumed he was out at a party. At ten-thirty she went to bed with a paperback and read for an hour, without really comprehending the story she was reading. She felt not only lonesome but afraid, all alone in the cottage.

She hadn't been scared before, though she supposed there was some danger in being alone in the cottage, which was rather isolated. Tomorrow night she would bring Brix over to protect her. The dog wouldn't howl if she were let into the cottage, and it would be nice having something of Kurt's nearby.

Chapter Seven

Thursday morning the sun was back in the sky, gleaming palely through the covering mist. The landscape looked newly washed after the rainfall. Trees shone in the filtered light, and the beach was a bonanza of driftwood, seaweed, stones and shells. The tractors cleaned the beach in the tourist resort areas, but on this lonesome stretch the debris was left for the beachcombers. It was one of Shawna's favorite beach activities, and she wasn't alone.

Joe and Josh Brown and Brix accompanied her as she went foraging for pretty shells and pebbles to add to her collection. Every year she collected a mound of seashells. One of these years, she would think of something artistic to do with it.

Shawna offered to drive Sally to the restaurant again for lunch. But Sally had a different idea. "I want to help Ed clean the kitchen. Would you mind running herd on the boys for a few hours this afternoon?''

"I'd be happy to.''

Shawna thought she might find an opportunity to search Kurt's cottage while Sally was away, but it wasn't possible. The boys stuck like glue. They were at that rambunctious age where they weren't quiet for a minute, and Shawna decided the safest place for them was outside of Kurt's cottage. She took them for a drive, bought them ice-cream cones at Kennebunkport, and finally returned to the cottage just as Sally was arriving.

Sally's mother was with her, and again Shawna felt she'd be in the way if she hung around, so she went back to her own cottage. She took out the Windsurfer and plunged into the cool sea. The wind was stiff, and she skimmed along the water's surface parallel to shore, but didn't tackle the tricky turn at Lighthouse Point. It was a dangerous stunt to attempt alone.

The phone rang at six, just as she was preparing dinner. Shawna ran excitedly to answer it, expecting to hear Kurt's voice. She felt a stab of disappointment when Everett spoke.

"I saw Slater in town today,'' he said excitedly. "This is your chance to search for my designs. Or have you already done it?''

She explained about the friends using the cottage. "It doesn't look like I'm going to be able to do it, Everett,'' she said.

"They must leave the house sometime.''

"I imagine they'll lock the door if they do,'' she said, looking at Kurt's key, gleaming from its spot on the kitchen counter. Why was she being so recalcitrant? Her mother had advised her not to do it, and she usually found her mother a pretty good adviser. But the real reason was a matter of the heart: she didn't want to prove Kurt had done something so despicable.

"I didn't think, when you left New York, that a little thing like a lock was going to stop you," Everett taunted. "What's changed your mind? As if I didn't know! You've been chummying up to Slater!"

"We've been out a few times," she admitted. "He seems like a really nice man, Everett."

"The slinky blonde on his arm at dinner last night seemed to feel the same way. She was all over him."

Shawna stiffened in alarm. Was Everett lying? "What time was this, Everett?" she asked.

"He arrived at Sardi's around nine."

Kurt had called her at nine-thirty. Had he called from the restaurant and said he was at home alone, missing her? "Are you sure?"

"Don't be ridiculous. I can produce witnesses, if you've decided not to trust me," Everett snapped.

As far as Shawna knew, Everett had never lied to her. "Of course I trust you," she replied. Guilt tweaked at her. She'd known Everett forever. Whom should she trust more—Uncle Max, or a man she'd only met a few days ago? A man that she already suspected of stealing.

"It was the new European model, Nadia. The word around town is that he's signing her to an exclusive contract. She's a beautiful woman. Quite elegant."

"Yes, I've seen her picture. She's—lovely." A pain burned in her chest to think of Kurt with that exotic creature with a lion's mane of golden, tousled hair and a sinuous body.

"She's a man-eater, but Slater won't mind that. He hardly took his eyes off her."

"Oh." It was a quiet, sad syllable, said to fill the void of silence.

"So, do you think you might get into the cottage before he returns to Maine?" Everett asked, suddenly businesslike.

Shawna bit back the tears and answered in the same voice. "I'll do my damnedest, Everett. I have a pretty good idea where to look. He keeps his cabinet locked."

"Then there's obviously something valuable in it."

"It looks that way. If necessary, I'll devise some ruse to lure the visitors away from the cottage. I'll call you tomorrow."

"I'll be waiting. Good luck."

"Bye."

Shawna hung up the phone and walked purposefully to the window that gave her a view of Kurt's cottage. The lights were on, indicating that Sally was still there. How could she get them all out of the house for half an hour? That was all the time she needed.

Suddenly, a plan took shape in her mind. She went to the phone and dialed Kurt's cottage. Sally answered on the second ring. "Hello?"

"How would you like a baby-sitter tonight, Sally?" Shawna offered. "You and Ed can go out somewhere and forget your troubles for a few hours. I'll put the kids to bed for you." And once they were in bed, she would have the downstairs to herself.

"Oh, thanks, Shawna, that's really nice of you to offer, but my mom's here. We're all going back to Wells Beach with her in a couple of hours. Why don't you come over for a cup of coffee before we go?"

Shawna knew she would be poor company. "I was just starting dinner," she said, hesitantly. She felt a prick of impatience for them to leave. As soon as the cottage was empty, she would go over and search.

"Maybe some other time then. Thanks for the offer anyway," Sally added before she hung up.

It was time to think of dinner, though Shawna wasn't really very hungry. Instead, she took a can of soda and her book out to the porch, where she could watch for the Browns' departure. It seemed like the hand of fate that they had decided to leave. Early evening dimmed to twilight, and Shawna gave up the pretense of reading. She just sat, staring out at the ocean, as it darkened from gray to black, glazed with the rays of the setting sun. The shadows on the beach were tinged with purple. She took the surfboard back to Wells Beach, came home and waited.

She'd search the cottage as soon as it was empty, then leave for New York tonight. Night driving didn't bother her. There would be less traffic. Sleep wouldn't come easily tonight anyway. If she slept at all, she'd dream of Kurt and Nadia, with her lion's mane and her lioness's appetite. Was he running his fingers through her tousled curls? Was he telling her she was beautiful? He didn't call her tonight, she noticed. It was nine o'clock. Last night he'd called at nine-thirty. The phone could be heard through the open door, but it didn't ring.

Soon Sally and Ed came out with the boys, everyone carrying luggage. Sally's mother was with them. They were all leaving!

Before she got in the car, Sally came flying down the beach, and Shawna went out to meet her.

"We're going down to Mom's," Sally said. "She's got a few days off work, so she's going to mind the kids while I give Ed a hand at the restaurant. I wanted to thank you for everything before I go."

"I didn't do anything. I wish there was something I could do."

"Come to the clambake." Sally laughed. "It'll be in a couple of weeks' time, right here at Kurt's cottage. Oh, and will you tell Kurt I'm sorry Josh broke the milk jug? I'll replace it."

"I'm sure he won't mind."

Sally looked over her shoulder, where her mother was standing by the car, waiting. "I've got to run. Gee, I wish we could have gotten to know each other better. But as you can see, this is kind of a busy time for me. Goodbye, Shawna."

They put their arms around each other and gave a final hug. The boys waved, and soon everyone was piling into the car. Shawna waved goodbye as they left. Then she went into Spindrift Cottage and got Kurt's key and her camera. Her jaw was set in a grim square as she trudged purposefully along the beach.

There was one other creature she had to say goodbye to, and she went around to see Brix before going inside. Kurt would be home by noon tomorrow. If Shawna took Brix for a run now and gave her fresh food and water, Kurt could feed her when he arrived.

He had explained that he flew into Portland, and drove up from there.

Brix leaped eagerly at her, licking her hands as she unfastened the collar. Poor Brix, she was lonesome, too. Shawna didn't bother with a leash. She knew Brix would only run along the beach. Brix was soon nosing in the sand for hidden clams. Every piece of seaweed and every bit of debris interested the dog. She carried several of them to Shawna as if they were presents. When the dog had had a good romp, Shawna took her back to the house and tied her up.

"So long, Brix," she said. On impulse, she bent down and hugged the dog around the neck. "You're a nice girl. You take care of him for me."

Brix barked her agreement, and it was time to begin the search. Brix continued barking after she left, trying to lure her back. With a deep sense of foreboding, Shawna took the key from her pocket and went around to the front door. She let herself in and turned on the lights. The familiar room sprang into view, looking just as she'd first seen it from outside the window Sunday evening, except, of course, that now Kurt wasn't at the drawing board. She closed the curtain, in case anyone passed by and saw her.

Her nerves were drawn taut as wire. Once the curtains were closed, she had the eerie feeling the house itself was watching her. That was what made her fingers shake, and not the dread of what she would find in the locked cabinet. When Brix stopped barking, the silence seemed ominous. But she had to get on with it.

Shawna tried the cabinet, in case Kurt had left it unlocked. When the door didn't budge, she began looking for the key. It would be small, like a suitcase or filing-cabinet key. Suddenly, she remembered the ring of keys in the kitchen. When she turned on the light to get it, Brix began barking again, but stopped when she returned to the living room. The key slid into the lock and turned easily.

Shawna's heart pounded in excitement. She was looking at Kurt's designs for next spring's show. They sat in a pile, each signed with his flourishing "Slater," and the date. She lifted one after the other, and a gasp of pleasure greeted each design. They were a radical departure from last year's style. Kurt had opted for a flowing, romantic line that showed off the female form. In the evening gowns, the waists were nipped, with flaring billows of skirt below. The suits were more feminine, too, with smaller shoulders and again tight waists, but the skirts were pencil thin.

Driven by pure curiosity, she shuffled quickly through them, noticing that Kurt certainly hadn't borrowed anything from Everett for this line. They were marvelous, but there was no need to photograph them. If he didn't win the Golden Needle again, Shawna would be surprised. But this wasn't what she'd come for. She set the sketches aside and rooted through other papers below.

There were other discarded sketches, some with a big X stroked through them. Many of the papers weren't designs at all, but drawings of the beach and of children playing there, sometimes with Brix. He had even sketched his dune buggy, with a long-legged woman standing beside it, laughing. It looked like Sally. This must have been done the day he gave Joe and Josh a ride in Nellie. Lower in the pile, Shawna recognized the face of a popular fashion model with a sailboat in the background, and felt a twinge of jealousy. Idiot, she told herself. Did you think you were the only one he ever entertained here?

She set these aside, too, and reached for a brown folder at the very bottom of the shelf. None of the other drawings were in folders, which indicated this lot had some unusual significance. Her fingers shook as she opened the folder. Right on top were half a dozen of Everett's sketches, the ones Kurt had stolen and altered for the autumn line that had won him the award.

A pervasive feeling of doom came over her, and she just sat, staring for a long time. Everett's accusations were all true then. Kurt was a thief. She flipped through the pages and found even more damning evidence. The sketches below showed clearly where Kurt had altered the designs. Shoulders were widened and the trim was changed to lighten Everett's formality to a less structured look, but the similarities were too close and too conclusive to deny the obvious.

Shawna sat back on her heels, thinking. The heavy silence was interrupted by a spate of barking from Brix. But she soon stopped, and Shawna assumed it was only someone passing on the beach, or the road above. Everett had told her not to take the sketches, just to take pictures of them. Shawna laid the pictures out on the sofa to photograph them. She would have to phone Everett as soon as she got back to the cottage. She was standing in front of the sofa, focusing the camera on the squares of white paper when Kurt appeared in the doorway.

Shawna was living a nightmare. This couldn't possibly be happening; Kurt was in New York. But it *was* happening. How had he gotten in? She would have heard him at the front door, so he must have come in by the back. That was why Brix had barked! And Kurt had come slipping in so quietly, almost as though he knew... All this flashed through her mind in seconds while they stood, staring mutely at each other.

Kurt's face looked frozen. It was even the color of ice, gray and pale. "Maybe you'd like to tell me what you're doing," he said, in a menacing voice she hardly recognized. His eyes skimmed from her guilty face, to the pictures laid out on the sofa, to the camera. "Or would that be redundant?"

Why should she feel guilty? *He* was the one who had been caught red-handed. "Just what you think," she answered. Her voice echoed his demeanor—hard and icy.

Kurt's nostrils flared dangerously, and for a minute she thought he would strike her. He was using all his willpower to control the urge. He stiffened like a statue, and there were traces of grim forbearing in the lines of his face. And yet, he couldn't control his eyes. Shawna had a fleeting thought of the ocean in a storm. His eyes held that same quality of swirling currents and raging tides, turmoil that could erupt at any moment and drown you.

A tremor shook him from head to toe. When he finally spoke, she could hear that he was on the verge of explosion. "Get out of my house," he said in a low, menacing growl.

Shawna hesitated. To leave, she would have to walk past him, and she was afraid of what he might do. Kurt took three jerky steps toward her, pulled the camera from her hands and opened it. He yanked out the film and unwound it, then flung it and the camera aside. "And don't ever come back."

As the shock waned, Shawna felt her reeling mind settle down. How dare he speak to her like that? She lifted her chin high and spat the words at him. "Destroying the film won't help, Slater."

"Tell your friend Everett for me if he ever tries it again, I'll have him arrested. When Nancy told me who you were, I didn't believe her. I thought you were different from the others, someone really special. You're no different. You just play the game a little rougher, no holds barred."

"I don't play games. I came here on business, and I found what I wanted."

"So you admit you came down here to seduce me!"

"*Seduce* you?" Shawna stared in astonishment. "I would have preferred it if I could have done this without ever speaking to you. Seeing you was a necessary evil."

Kurt's face was a mask of cynicism. "If that's true, you've missed your calling. Tell Everett if he uses as much as one of my designs, I'll bleed him dry. I can forgive an old man once. I'm compassionate; I'm not a sucker. How much was he paying you? Thirty pieces of silver?"

Shawna stared, trying to make sense of his ranting. "Why would he steal your designs? And I didn't do it for money! How dare you imply—"

"Oh, and what was the reason? Love?" he asked ironically.

"Yes, love of justice! Don't bother mounting your high horse with me, Slater. I know what you are, and before I'm done, the rest of the world will know, too.

I hope you enjoyed your award, because it's the last one you'll be winning."

Kurt's eyes narrowed suspiciously. He was silent a moment, trying to figure out her speech. When he spoke, his voice was contemptuous. "Well, that's an interesting excuse. I might have known a clever actress like you would have her lines rehearsed. So *I'm* the culprit, am I?"

She listened, weighing his insinuations. "Are you trying to deny it, when I have the evidence right in front of me?"

Kurt shook his head. "There's no point in bluffing. We both know what's going on. I grant you Everett was good once. But he's over the hill now, he's had it. I'd advise him to retire with dignity, or I'll retire him—in court. You tell him that for me."

"You're the one who had *his* sketches. He didn't have *yours*. We'll see who takes whom to court!" Shawna snatched up her camera and headed for the door.

Kurt grabbed her arm as she passed and swung her around. As he studied her pale, frightened face, with the green eyes blinking, he felt a weakening stab of pity, or love. Shawna was young, and impressionable. Everett must have been taking advantage of her. Maybe he had some hold over her, something from the past that he was using as blackmail. "Why did you do it?" he asked. "Why did you really do it? Nancy told me your mother is Adele." He paused, questioningly, waiting. He could understand a woman protecting her mother, if that was the explanation.

"What's that got to do with anything? My mother begged me not to come here."

His eyes blazed with frustration. "Was it for money? Ambition? Did Everett promise to advance your career? You chose the wrong man. He's on the decline."

Shawna wrenched her arm free. "My career will advance based on the merits of my talent. I came here because I don't like cheats, Slater. If Everett's so old hat, why did you steal from him?"

Kurt's grim face assumed a contemptuous tinge. "So you're sticking to that story. You make it pretty hard for me to forgive you."

"Forgive me?" she gasped.

"If you don't convince me Everett took advantage of you, you're in a bad jam. Breaking and entering is a serious crime."

"I didn't break and enter. You'll find your key in the kitchen."

"Betraying our friendship isn't indictable, of course. A mere lapse of morals." His eyes flickered over her, dismissing her. "That certainly wouldn't bother someone like you."

Shawna felt her hackles rise at his degrading tone. "There's nothing wrong with my morals."

"You practically admitted you came here to seduce me. What held you back?"

"Revulsion!" she shot back.

His fingers pressed ruthlessly into her arms, and the sea of his eyes was turbulent. Shawna felt she was drowning in their slate-green depths. "Would it be worse than prison?" His eyes slid to the telephone. His painful hold on her arms first lessened, then he released her.

Shawna put her hand on her hip as an expression of disdain settled on her face. "Go ahead. I have nothing to fear."

Kurt felt his blood rise at her defiant stance. "Don't be too sure. I *did* unwittingly destroy the evidence," he said, looking at the spoiled film, "but I'm not without influence in our profession. I could have you barred from ever setting foot in a design house again. You wouldn't be allowed to sweep the floors, and certainly not to empty the waste baskets, with the habit your sticky fingers have picked up. We designers often discard a rough sketch."

"Is that what you had Nancy Alton do, Slater? No, of course not. You're too fastidious for that. You wanted a good clear copy, so you wouldn't miss any details."

"You really should study Nancy's case. She had a tough time getting a job when Everett was through with her. But then, she didn't agree to spy for him, of course. I'm sure you'll fare better, Shawna. You'll land on your feet, no matter what I decide to do about Everett stealing my designs."

Shawna felt a spasm of uncertainty. She had always found it hard to believe Kurt would steal. The new sketches she had looked at were certainly his own. Everett had nothing remotely similar to them. Why would a designer as talented as Kurt pirate someone else's creations? And if he didn't . . . But he had Everett's sketches, done in Everett's own hand. He *had* to be a thief!

"What are Everett's designs doing in your cottage, if you didn't have them stolen?"

"I was gathering evidence against him, with Nancy's help. She brought them to me the day she left Everett. I analyzed them and decided to give him the benefit of the doubt, and wait to see if his next line was also derivative. That's the polite word we use to mean stolen."

Shawna swallowed her confusion. "I don't believe you," she said.

Kurt gave a shrug of indifference, but the angry spark in his eyes belied it. "Frankly, I don't give a damn what you believe. You're either a naive fool or Everett's accomplice. You just give him my message. I'm serving notice. Next season, if he dishes up my designs with his belts and buttons, I'll sue."

Shawna bit her lip in indecision. Her mind was overwhelmed with doubts. If what Kurt said was true, she had torpedoed her own career before it got afloat, but worse, she had wrongly accused Kurt. And even worse, she had betrayed him by ransacking his house, after he'd entrusted the key to her.

Kurt watched as she considered all this. "Second thoughts?" he jeered. "A tricky business, changing horses in midstream."

She reached instinctively for his hand. "Kurt, if I was wrong..."

Kurt shook off her hand. He didn't want to touch her, or he might end up forgiving her, and the pain of her deception was too new for that. "You *were* wrong, Shawna. I thought we knew each other well enough that we could tell the truth. If you had any doubts about me, why didn't you just ask? After we became friends, I mean."

She shook her head in frustration. "How could I?"

"Is telling the truth actually impossible for you? I confessed that I wasn't a commercial artist. That might have been a suitable time. My God, I actually felt guilty about that innocent deception, and all the time you were deceiving me and laughing."

"I didn't enjoy it!" she said. Tears stung her eyes. "I *wanted* to ask you."

"But you didn't. You'd rather make love with a man you thought was a thief and a liar than confront him with the truth. I don't know what I ever saw in you."

Her anger hardened again at his rejection, and she shouted back, "I had no intention of making love with you! I just did what I had to do." She turned and marched toward the door, half expecting Kurt to chase after her. When he didn't, she stopped and turned back. "And furthermore," she added haughtily, "I don't believe a word you said. I'm going to tell Everett what I found here. You'll be hearing from his lawyers in the morning."

"See you in court."

She opened the door and strode out into the cool night air, which seemed like an icy whip against her fevered cheeks. The sea was a vast body of calm darkness, stretching to infinity. Brix barked when she heard the front door slam. It was somehow the last straw. Hot tears burned Shawna's eyes as she ran back to Spindrift Cottage.

Inside, she looked at the phone and thought of Everett, but she was too upset to phone him yet. First she wanted to go over what Kurt had said and see if she could make sense of it. The chief stumbling block to believing him was that he had Everett's designs. He said Nancy Alton had given them to him. Maybe she should call Nancy Alton.

After she had calmed down, she got Nancy's number from the operator and called her. "Nancy, this is Shawna Cassidy. I work for Maxwell Everett," she said.

"Of course, Kurt and I were talking about you today," Nancy replied. Her voice was stiff with disapproval. "What is it you want, Miss Cassidy?"

Shawna hesitated, taken aback by the gruff tone of Nancy's voice. "I wanted to ask you about some designs in Kurt Slater's possession that belong to Maxwell Everett. Kurt told me you had given them to him."

"Yes, I did," Nancy answered unhesitatingly.

"Why?"

"Because I thought Kurt had the right to know he was being ripped off. I saw the original collection Everett was preparing for that season. It was nothing like the designs he suddenly came up with two weeks before the show. I knew he'd gotten hold of somebody else's sketches. It wasn't the first time," she added in a hard voice, "but on other occasions it was only one or two outfits."

"How could he have gotten Kurt's designs?"

"He bought photographs of them for five thousand dollars from George Haines, one of Kurt's employees. I did some spying on my own, and found Kurt's designs in Everett's desk drawer, the signature still intact. That sort of trick reflects on the whole company. I didn't intend to let Everett destroy my name."

Shawna's heart felt heavy. "Thank you for telling me. But why didn't you report Everett and this George Haines?"

"I left that up to Kurt. Haines was asked to resign—*I* would have fired him. Kurt decided to give Everett another chance. I think he felt sorry for him— Max is no longer a young go-getter. Kurt didn't want to create a scandal in the industry, although rumors got out, of course, when I quit and later joined Slater's studio."

"Quit? I thought Everett fired you!"

Nancy made a scoffing noise. "I wouldn't work for Everett if he paid me a million dollars. And I suggest you bale out, Miss Cassidy, before he ruins your career."

"It looks as though he's already done that," Shawna said.

"Then you *did* agree to spy on Slater for him? I heard from an old friend at Everett's that you were vacationing in Maine. I wondered about it, and decided to warn Kurt when he was in town today. Kurt was sure it was just a coincidence, but apparently you weren't exactly truthful about who you are."

"I was misinformed about a few things. I agreed to help Everett find out if Kurt was pilfering his designs. That's the story Everett told me," Shawna admitted.

Nancy Alton's voice had begun to lose its hard edge. When she spoke again, it bore a trace of pity. "Please don't tell Everett anything about Kurt's new spring and summer line. I know you saw the sketches. I was talking to Kurt not five minutes ago."

"That's not what I was looking for in his house!"

"But you saw them?"

"Yes," Shawna admitted in a small voice. "But I wasn't going to tell Everett. I was just looking for evidence that Kurt had stolen his designs. That's all."

"Everett's as shifty as a rattlesnake," Nancy said disdainfully. "The pirating scam was just an excuse. He knew Kurt was working on his new collection at his cottage. What he really hoped was that you'd come across those sketches, so that he could pick your brain clean."

"Do you really think Everett would do that?" Shawna asked.

"Try him."

"Maybe I will. Thanks for your help, Nancy."

"That's all right. I didn't want to see Kurt get hurt, and it was pretty obvious he was head over heels in love with you."

Shawna winced at the words, but didn't want to reveal her vulnerability. "Really?" she asked, trying for a nonchalant tone. "I heard he was dating Nadia, the new European model."

"Nadia Jirat? She flew back to Europe a week ago. Kurt interviewed her for an assignment, but they couldn't come to terms. He didn't feel she was quite right for his style. The minute Kurt's seen with a woman, the meeting is blown into a love affair. Once people even thought that Kurt and I were an item. My fiancé certainly didn't appreciate that!"

Nancy Alton had no reason to lie to Shawna about Nadia, but Everett did. Just as he'd told her Kurt and Nancy were romantically involved. Afraid that she was falling for Kurt, Uncle Max had lied to anger her, and to get her back on his side. He had manipulated her very skillfully, and she'd fallen into his trap.

"I must have been mistaken. I heard he was out with her last night."

"No, he was home. He called me around nine, and said he was sending out for pizza. Where'd you hear that?"

"Everett told me."

"I thought so. Are you beginning to get the picture, Shawna?"

"Yes, I guess I am. Thanks for talking to me, Nancy."

"That's all right."

After a moment of silence, Nancy asked, "Any message for Kurt? I'll be seeing him tomorrow at the office."

Shawna bit her lips to steady them. "Tell him I'm sorry," she said. "Bye, Nancy."

She hung up the receiver and reviewed the situation. It was true Everett had made a point of asking her to photograph Kurt's new line, using the excuse that some of his sketches had been stolen. But that was probably a lie, too.

Reluctantly, she dialed Everett's number. He picked up on the third ring. "Hello?"

"I got into Kurt's house," she said, then waited with bated breath.

"Good! Did you find any evidence?"

"Yes, he had your sketches all right."

"I knew it! What else did you see?"

In his eagerness, Everett didn't even bother claiming any interest in the evidence. "What do you mean?" Shawna asked.

"What's his new line like? You haven't forgotten that two of my sketches were stolen from my apartment?"

"Which sketches, Everett? Gowns, I think you said?"

"Yes, two evening gowns. What are Slater's evening gowns like?"

"What were yours like?" she parried. "The ones that were stolen, I mean?"

"They were strapless. Is Slater's evening line strapless?"

"No, I guess he isn't using yours after all."

"Well, what are his like? Are they full, fitted, what?"

"What difference does it make?" she asked innocently. "He isn't using your sketches. Are you sure they were stolen? Maybe you misplaced them."

"They were stolen. You'd better get right back, Shawna. You got pictures of everything?"

"I snapped pictures of those designs of yours that he had. That's what you wanted, isn't it? Evidence?"

"You mean you didn't take pictures of his *new* line? How am I going to be sure he isn't copying me again? I think you'd better run back to his place before he comes home and take pictures of everything."

"He's already back, Everett."

There was an abrupt silence. "Come on back to New York right away. We'll talk."

"I don't think so. I won't be returning to the House of Everett. I don't care for the way you handle your business. I've been talking to Nancy Alton. You used me! You didn't want evidence against Kurt. You just wanted me to look at his new designs and carry home his ideas for you to steal again. How *could* you? You were like an uncle to me!" The tears streamed down her face.

"Shawna, don't be absurd. You don't know what you're saying. This is your old Uncle Max."

"Not any longer. Goodbye, *Mr.* Everett."

She hung up the receiver and breathed a deep sigh. There, it was done. She was through with Maxwell Everett. Let Kurt sue him. She wouldn't blame him one bit. Shawna went out to the porch and looked down the beach toward Kurt's cottage. The lights were on, but she'd closed the curtains herself, so she wouldn't be able to see Kurt. Her memories would have to sustain her.

Kurt sat staring at the pictures arranged on his sofa. Shawna had been photographing Everett's sketches, but that didn't mean she hadn't photographed the new spring and summer line first. That sweet face that looked so innocent, so sincere. Boy, he'd really been taken in by her act. She found him revolting. He scooped up the sketches, put them in the cupboard and locked the door. Then he went out to bring Brix in for company. Popping open a can of beer, he sat down at his drafting board. The sketch of Shawna in the sea-foam green gown was covered with layers of paper. He removed them and stood, gazing at the illustration.

Setting the beer aside, he grabbed the drawing and squashed it into a ball. "Come on, Brix. You and I need some exercise."

He opened the door and went out to walk along the beach.

Chapter Eight

That night, in a state of chaos, Shawna packed up her car and returned to New York. It was a long, exhausting trip, and when she finally arrived she fell into bed, too weary to think. It wasn't until morning that the full scope of the debacle became clear. In one stroke she had lost the man she loved, thrown over her job and seriously damaged her future. She had always looked up to Everett, and his betrayal was a deep sorrow. How had she been taken in by him?

He was always egotistical, but she had put it down to the artistic temperament. With flunkies bowing and scraping, it seemed only natural that his head would be a little big. Everett lived in the past, that was his trouble. His style of designing wasn't popular any longer. His clients were mostly wealthy, aging matrons. The gowns he designed would soon belong in a museum.

He had belittled her work from the beginning. "No elegance, Shawna," he'd chided. But sportswear wasn't supposed to be elegant. Maybe it was a good thing he never used her designs for his sportswear line. He would have imposed his old-fashioned ideas on her modern work, and the results would have been disastrous.

Everett's pride couldn't accept failure or even the changing tides of fashion. When even the formal style changed from what he knew, he had just plain stolen ideas from the most talented designer around, Slater. Had Kurt been referring to Everett when he said some people couldn't accept failure? And she had voiced her objections so vehemently, thinking he was excusing himself. It was one more small humiliation to be endured.

Kurt... Her thoughts roamed to the more recent past. "It was pretty obvious that he was head over heels in love with you," Nancy had said. The last time Shawna saw him, it had been abundantly clear that he despised her.

Shawna dragged herself out of bed like a zombie. After a shower, she felt revived enough to make coffee and try to plan her day. To even consider the rest of her life was too depressing. *Take it one day at a time—just survive,* she told herself. One unpleasant task looming before her was the trip to Everett's studio, to clean out her office. Would Kurt have his lawyers there, or the police?

Curiosity urged her to dash over to Seventh Avenue at once, but dread held her back. At eleven-thirty, she dressed and took a taxi to the office. Everett's door was closed, but he was in. She wouldn't go in to see him. She never wanted to see him again. The work she'd done for Everett belonged to him, and there wasn't much to take away, just the personal things from her desk, items that fit into one canvas bag. Shawna took a last look around. As it was nearly noon, the others were beginning to leave for lunch.

They didn't appear to suspect that anything was wrong, A few of them asked what she was doing back in the middle of her vacation. "Just couldn't stay away, huh?" She managed a weak smile. When they were gone, she glanced back at Everett's door. A spurt of anger impelled her toward it. She wouldn't let him off so easily. Why not tell him what she thought of him? She marched determinedly toward the tall oak door and knocked once before entering.

Her anger evaporated when she saw Everett slumped over his desk with his head in his hands. She thought he had been crying. He looked like an old, ruined man. The face that she remembered as being aristocratic and chiseled was now riddled with devastation.

"I'm ruined," he said, nervously fingering a dark red silk handkerchief. "What can I say, Shawna? I shouldn't have dragged you into this mess. Adele will never forgive me. I'm sorry, my dear."

Her anger faded until she could only feel sorry for him. "Oh, Uncle Max, why did you do it?" she asked.

"Greed, avarice, but mostly plain old pride. It hurt to see my work being ignored. I thought that if I could bring out one more really stunning collection, things would be the way they used to be. I'd be back on top again. But it didn't work out that way. Slater's style couldn't be altered successfully. There's an integrity to his designs...." Everett drew a long, sad breath.

"You didn't have any sketches stolen by Slater at all, did you, Everett? It was just a ruse to learn what his new line was like."

"It was the act of a desperate man," he admitted. When he met her gaze, she saw fear in his eyes—fear mingled with grief and disappointment. "What do you think Slater will do?" he asked.

"I don't know," Shawna answered. "He was furious last night. He said he had been willing to forgive once, but this time I think he means to make trouble."

"My God, I'll be ruined! My whole reputation shattered. Can't you talk to him?"

The very idea sent Shawna into shock. "I'm the *last* person he'd listen to. He hates me!"

"I had the idea you two were getting along pretty well."

"Is that why you told me he was out with Nadia, to upset me? It wasn't true, was it, Everett?"

"I just repeated gossip."

"You said you *saw* them! You even described how they were behaving."

"I didn't want you getting involved with him, but since you were on close terms, it might work to our advantage."

"We're not on close terms now. That was before..." She let her words trail off.

Everett's head rose, and when he spoke again, the pride was creeping back into his voice. "I won't go begging for mercy. I don't think he can prove anything. I still have friends in this business. Slater's a parvenu. People will listen to me.''

"Oh, Everett," she said angrily, "your best chance is just to tell him you're sorry, and promise you won't do it again. I think maybe he'll be willing to overlook it. He's really very...kind," she said, carefully choosing the word. It seemed the right choice. Kurt had been kind to Ed and Sally.

"You want me to go crawling to that—"

"I didn't say crawl. Just apologize."

Everett's nostrils pinched, and his old haughty look was firmly back in place. "Everett crawls to no one," he said.

His mood reactivated all of Shawna's fury. He hadn't learned anything. He wasn't even sorry, except that he'd gotten caught. Her eyes blazed. "You haven't changed a bit, have you?" she shouted fiercely. "Well, I'll tell you this, Everett. You'd better get down off your high horse and apologize in private, or the whole mess will be made public. All your colleagues will be laughing at you. It's up to you. I'm leaving now, and I won't be back."

Everett's eyes narrowed skeptically. He didn't even say goodbye when Shawna stormed out and slammed the door.

He was sitting in his office, alone, when the phone rang and a deep voice said, "This is Slater speaking. You and I have something to discuss, Mr. Everett. I'm in my office. I'll expect you right away."

"Of course, Mr. Slater," Everett said through clenched lips.

He rose stiffly from his chair and went to his private washroom to comb his hair and apply fresh cologne before leaving for the appointment.

The next thing Shawna learned about Everett was that he was closing his New York office and transferring his operations to Paris. The announcement was in the next morning's paper. There was no mention of Slater at all. Was Everett running away? Had he spoken to Kurt? Would *she* end up being the one sued?

Shawna called Everett's secretary, but didn't learn much. "Everett had been planning the move for some time," the secretary said. "I'm staying behind a month to close down things here. I'll be joining Everett in Paris soon. Your check will be in the mail, Shawna, and if you want a letter of reference, there's one here. Everett signed it before he left."

"I never heard him mention Paris."

"It's a logical move. Everett's style has always been more appreciated in Europe. Most of his customers are there. It was a toss-up between Paris and Rome. He finally settled on Paris."

Shawna cleared her throat nervously and said, "Did he mention anything about Kurt Slater, before he left?"

"Slater? No, he didn't. Why do you ask?"

"I just thought he might have—said something."

"That'd be a good house for you to apply to, Shawna. Why don't you call Slater and set up an appointment?"

The ironic suggestion indicated that the secretary had no idea what was going on. Shawna thanked her and said goodbye. But the suggestion also reminded her she'd have to find another position. Not much could be done about it on a Saturday, but she spent the weekend assembling her portfolio and updating her résumé. Naturally she couldn't submit it to Slater. She'd get on with her career where she should have begun in the first place, at one of the smaller, more progressive houses.

She tried to think of Kurt as Slater, to put some distance between them. That was the way she would have to think of him in the future. He was no longer her friend and neighbor, but a colleague, whom she had plenty of reasons to fear.

After a week of interviews, Shawna concluded that Everett's crime was going to remain a secret. None of the designers who interviewed her made any sly comments. She noticed that association with the House of Everett was neither a bonus nor a drawback. Working for Everett wasn't the prestigious experience it would have been ten or twenty years ago, but the name was still fairly respectable.

On Thursday she landed an interview at Renfrews. The house was a small but promising one, which was beginning to expand. It was run by Irene Renfrew, a striking woman in her late thirties. She was more stylish than actually pretty. Her black hair hung in a wedge around her slender face, and she wore huge red-rimmed glasses.

"Why did you join Everett's house?" Irene asked, scanning Shawna's portfolio. "This hardly seems like his sort of thing."

"He was planning to expand into a casual line, but his removal to Paris brought that to a halt," she explained uneasily.

Irene examined the portfolio carefully. "I like this full-backed jacket. You have a knack with knitted materials." She set the sketch aside and smiled at a pair of pleated slacks. "These are good. The wide waistband gives them a certain style. Hmm."

After half an hour's discussion, Shawna was offered a position. She left, walking on air. Renfrews was the kind of house where she belonged. Irene appreciated her designs. Perhaps she had a future in the fashion industry after all.

All week Shawna had been so busy job-hunting that she'd managed to shove Kurt Slater to the back of her mind. Of course, she thought of him often, but her memories were so painful that she tried to keep them at bay. Unfortunately, on Saturday she had nothing planned. As she sat at breakfast, she was inundated with regrets. It was a relief that she'd gotten another position, but that didn't assuage the loneliness, or the ache of remorse.

Was Kurt in New York, or was he back in Maine? As she looked out at the sunny sky, she wished she were still at Spindrift Cottage. Then she was sorry she'd even gone there in the first place. At least Kurt hadn't made any trouble for Everett, and for that she was grateful. Had Everett merely run away, hoping to avoid prosecution? The dread was always at the back of her mind that Kurt could still sue her for her part in the fiasco.

The weekend loomed so uninvitingly before her that Shawna thought she might go down and visit her mother in Connecticut. They had spoken on the phone about Everett's sudden move to Paris, but Shawna hadn't gone into detail about her trip to Maine, except to say that Everett had been mistaken to think Slater was stealing his designs. She'd wanted to make that clear.

"I never believed it for a moment," Adele had said firmly. "He was always paranoid. I'm glad you didn't get involved in it."

Shawna was just reaching for the phone to call her mother when it rang. "It's Irene, Shawna," the familiar voice said. "Are you busy this evening?"

Thinking that her new boss might have something work-related in mind, Shawna immediately canceled her plans to go to Connecticut. "No, I'm free," she said.

"Good. I'm having a little party at my place tonight. A bunch of colleagues will be here. I should have invited you yesterday. It just occurred to me that you might like to come."

Since "little parties" were as important to the fashion industry as every moment spent in the design studio, Shawna would attend. "I'd love to," she agreed.

"Good. We're meeting around nine. Just drinks and conversation—and dancing if anyone has the strength. I live in a converted loft in Soho." She gave the address, and Shawna jotted it down.

"Bring an escort, if you like. It's strictly informal, and there's plenty of room."

"I'll see you at nine, Irene. Thanks."

The party gave Shawna something to look forward to, and lifted her from her dismal mood. She phoned a few old friends, trying to round up a date, but anyone who wasn't busy was out of town in the dead heat of summer. Oh, well, it was no crime to attend a party alone these days.

She cleaned her apartment and went grocery shopping in the morning, and met a friend at the health club to work out in the afternoon. In the summer, she couldn't face her regular exercises, but often went swimming. The quiet, pale green shimmer of the pool looked insignificant compared to the ocean. There was no danger here, only the sharp smell of chlorine.

Why was she thinking of the ocean so much lately? She had always loved it, but recently it seemed to beckon her. It was almost an obsession. The hazy striations from a hot sidewalk would bring the rolling waves to mind. When she was sitting on a bus or shopping, its great, billowing dark swells would suddenly loom up, so sharply it seemed like a mirage.

Sometimes she felt she was drowning in those billowing waves, other times they transformed magically into Kurt's stormy eyes. She would remember Kurt's red-and-white sail skimming over the waves, and even imagine the tangy smell of the sea. When she walked in the rain, the raindrops reminded her of spindrift blowing in her face.

The pool was an inadequate alternative, but she dived in and swam till her muscles ached, and the nervous tension had dissipated. Then she went home, tired but feeling better. Swimming gave her an appetite, and she wanted more than a sandwich for dinner. She had a sudden yen for seafood, lobster or clams.... More reminders of Kurt. Instead she had cold roast beef and a salad and drank two glasses of orange juice.

When it was time to prepare for Irene's party, Shawna fussed over her appearance. The guests were going to be designers and models in the fashion industry, so she wanted to look her best. As Irene had said the party was casual, Shawna decided to wear one of her own sporty designs.

Under the new, freer fashion rules, Shawna's red hair didn't prevent her from wearing pink, which was her favorite color. The evening was warm, and she chose a pair of full-legged glazed cotton pants and a short top that revealed a few inches of torso. A cool, breezy outfit might be welcome in the crowded room. Spiky rose kid sandals lent a festive accent to the outfit, and for the final touch, she wore a big pair of ivory hoop earrings.

Her short hair required nothing but a flick of the brush. The week in Maine had left her complexion with a healthy glow, so she didn't have to wear any makeup, except lipstick and eye shadow. When she was ready, she examined herself in the full-length mirror. The effect was good, but she'd have to remind herself to smile when she arrived at the party. The woman in the mirror seemed ready to burst into tears. Her green eyes were lackluster, her lips locked in a pout.

Shawna took a taxi to the loft, and followed a few other guests to the elevator. The hubbub of music and conversation and laughter echoed down the hall from Irene's open door. Shawna remembered to smile when Irene welcomed her at the door. She introduced Shawna to some of her other employees. As Shawna already knew some of the guests, she was soon mingling among them, distracted by the party.

Fashion parties were always interesting. The conversation centered around their work, and was liberally sprinkled with gossip. To Shawna's relief, Everett didn't figure too prominently in the latter. His departure was mentioned with a shrug. The younger crowd here already considered him history. Irene's loft was enviably large, but even its yawning cavity was soon crowded. A space was cleared in the middle of the living room for people to dance. Shawna stayed on the sidelines, talking, mostly getting to know her new workmates.

Irene served a buffet of tapas. "More than hors d'oeuvres, less than a meal," she explained. "They serve them in Spain before lunch, but there's no lunch to follow, folks. Dig in."

The menu was varied, with warm sweet curried oysters and cucumber sauce, beef bites sautéed with red peppers and snow peas, spiced with a fiery sauce, and mushroom caps stuffed with crab. Shawna made her selection and joined her friends. Everyone was raving about the food. Shawna acknowledged that it was delicious, and wondered why she was feeling so miserable.

She was at a fabulous party, making new friends and renewing acquaintance with old ones. The company was good, the food and wine excellent. So why did she feel as if she didn't have a friend in the world? Why did every piece of crab and every curried oyster remind her of Maine? Why was that headache closing so tightly against her temples?

It was the noise, she decided. Irene had the stereo turned up loud, and the babble of conversation added to the racket. She glanced at her watch. Eleven-thirty; she didn't like to leave before midnight. The party would go on till two or three. It seemed unfriendly to leave her boss's party so early, but if she didn't get away soon her head would split wide open.

She could say she had to leave for Connecticut early in the morning. It was her only choice. Shawna set her nearly full plate aside and went in search of Irene to say goodbye, and thank her for the party. As she worked her way through the throng, she spotted a slender woman with straw-blond hair, worn long. Nancy Alton! Her heart began hammering in her ears. Was Kurt here? She looked around the room, but didn't see him. It was all right then. Her pulse settled down to normal.

Before Shawna left she knew she should thank Nancy in person for her help in the Everett affair. "Nancy," she called, above the din.

Nancy turned and smiled. "Shawna!"

They moved aside, searching for a quiet corner. "I want to thank you for—you know," Shawna said, with a wince of embarrassment.

"That's all right. I didn't want to see your career ended before you even had a chance."

"Do you know anything about Everett's sudden flight to Paris?" Shawna asked.

Nancy laughed. "Not really, but I have my suspicions. He came to see Kurt last Friday."

"Really!"

Nancy lifted a brow and added, "By request, I believe. Didn't you know? Loud words were exchanged. That's probably why Kurt had him over during the lunch hour, so no one would hear. When I spotted Everett in the hall, I hung around, but couldn't make out exactly what they were saying."

"You shatter my faith in humanity," Shawna replied. "I was hoping Everett had the guts to go of his own accord. I advised him to."

"You're brave! Advising the Great Everett." Nancy glanced over Shawna's shoulder and waved. "Over here, Kurt," she called.

Shawna felt her blood turn to ice water. Kurt, here! She looked wildly for some means of escape, till she realized she was being as bad as Everett, trying to run away. It was time to face the music, but as far as she was concerned, the music was a death march. At that moment, she would rather have faced a firing squad than Kurt Slater.

Chapter Nine

Before Shawna had time to faint or melt into the floor, Kurt was standing beside Nancy. The shock of seeing him again in the flesh at close range, after all her imaginings, left her weak. Tonight he looked better than she'd ever seen him before. The casually elegant white linen jacket and textured gray jeans were the perfect outfit for the party. He wore them with an air of nonchalance, unaware of how striking he looked. The white was a dramatic contrast to his deep tan and dark hair.

When he saw Shawna, one of his highly arched eyebrows rose in derision, and the expression on his face was close to a sneer. "Miss Cassidy," he said, with a curt nod.

Shawna looked at him, and felt she had never known this cold, sneering man. "Hello, Kurt," she murmured. She should have called him Slater, since he was being so formal.

"Shawna and I have just been talking about Everett's abrupt departure," Nancy said.

"Can't we find something interesting to discuss?" Kurt asked in a bored tone. "Like the weather," he added, to show her that even that platitude was preferable to Maxwell Everett.

"Or food," Nancy suggested, looking toward the buffet. "I'm starved. This man's a slave driver," she said to Shawna, with a nod of her head to Kurt. "We've been sweating over a hot drawing board all evening, and he calls a hotdog bought on a street corner 'dinner.' I'm going to eat." She gave Shawna a conspiratory wink and walked away.

Shawna wanted to run after her, but she was determined to thank Kurt for not ruining her and Everett. She braced herself to deliver her speech. It would have helped if he didn't stand frozen like an iceberg, glowering at her. Tonight, his eyes were the cold, slate green of a stormy winter.

Shawna took a deep breath to steady her voice and forged on with her speech. "I want to thank you for not hauling Everett and me into court," she said stiffly. "Nancy told me about his visit to your office."

"We settled out of court," he replied, equally curt.

"Was it part of the deal that he go to Paris?"

"That was his own idea. He knew he was washed up here." Kurt turned his head aside and began scanning the room, as though he would like to leave. She examined his clean-cut profile. The strong nose and square jaw looked predatory and savage. He seemed so different from the gentle, caring man she'd known in Maine. This was the old "wine, women and song" Slater she was seeing tonight. It hurt to know she was responsible for his reversion.

After a moment, he looked at Shawna again and said, "Have you managed to find work?" There was a fierce glitter in his eyes, as if it required all his willpower just to be polite.

"I've joined Irene Renfrew. I start work Monday."

"I thought perhaps you'd be going to Paris, too," he said with a sneer.

Joining Everett was what he meant. "No, I'll be staying in New York. I think it'll work out better this way. At least Irene and I have the same ideas about fashion."

A flame leaped in his eyes, and his voice was harsh. "Why did you ever go to work for Everett in the first place?"

"He was an old family friend. At the time, I didn't know how he operated."

"You must have had *some* idea when he sent you down to *spy* on me!"

Kurt's voice was hoarse with anger. His control was slipping, and Shawna felt a quake building inside. He was going to berate her, right here at the party, in front of her new boss. In her worst imaginings, it had never come to this. "I thought you were the one who was stealing his designs," she reminded him.

"Thanks a lot!" he growled.

Shawna knew that if she didn't escape immediately, she was going to be publicly humiliated. Hot tears welled up in her eyes. Furious, she tried to blink them away.

"I said I'm sorry. I don't know what else I can say, or what you want me to do." She turned and hurried to the door. As Irene was nowhere in sight, she would have to phone her tomorrow and apologize for leaving without saying goodbye.

The door of the loft was still open. Some of the guests had spilled out into the hall to escape the heat and noise. Shawna saw only a teary blur of faces as she dashed toward the elevator. When she got there, it was on its way down, so she had to wait.

After peering at Kurt from the buffet table, Nancy walked back to join him. "I see you handled that like a true gentleman," she said, with a sardonic look.

Kurt's jaws were working to suppress his rage. "You could hardly expect me to congratulate her."

"Kurt, for heaven's sake, you weren't this hard on Everett. It wasn't Shawna's fault. She was taken in, like me. You don't beat the victim. She wasn't in cahoots with him, you know. And did you have to attack her here, at her boss's party?" She shook her head. "It's just not like you to be so insensitive."

Kurt was equally annoyed with himself. "I guess I lost my head. I'll go after her. She couldn't have gone far yet."

Nancy smiled with satisfaction as Kurt dashed toward the door. When he strode into the hall, the elevator door was just opening for more late-arriving guests. Before the door closed, he joined Shawna in the elevator.

She looked at him with dread. Now she was going to hear what he really thought of her, with no holds barred. The clang of the closing door reminded her of a prison. They were locked together in the little cage.

Although Shawna would rather have been locked up with a tiger, she tried to behave normally. She peered at Kurt from the side of her eyes, trying to gauge his mood. He looked grim, but didn't say anything.

"Leaving so soon?" she asked.

"I'm not leaving. I just came to apologize. I'm sorry I cut up at you in public. That was rude."

He was apologizing! The shock left her speechless for a moment. "It's all right," she said, when she'd recovered.

"No, it isn't. I behaved like a boor. I hope you aren't leaving the party early on my account."

"No, I was just on my way out when I bumped into Nancy."

"How are you getting home?"

In her haste, Shawna had overlooked this problem. "I'll find a taxi."

"On Saturday night? Lots of luck. I'll stay with you till you hail one. You shouldn't be on the streets alone."

Every minute with him was torment. Shawna tried to dissuade him, but Kurt wanted to make amends for his rudeness. He found that New York taxis came in two forms: occupied and off duty. For ten minutes they stood on the curb, waiting, flailing their arms, running into the road when they spotted an approaching taxi, but each time the cab flew past without even slowing.

"I'll have to drive you home," Kurt decided.

"No! I'll go back up and phone for a taxi."

"It wasn't much of a party anyway," Kurt said.

"Won't you have to take Nancy home?"

"Her fiancé's meeting her there later. I'm parked a few blocks away."

The last person in the world Shawna wanted to accept any favors from was Kurt Slater, but he insisted, and they walked along to the parking garage. Their conversation was limited to a few complaints about the heat.

"I thought you'd be back at the cottage by now," Shawna mentioned.

"I'm going tomorrow morning."

"Oh." No possibility of seeing him around town in the near future then. Not that it would have given Shawna any pleasure. The last half hour had been one of the most difficult of her life. Yet she was sorry to hear he was leaving. "Lucky you," she said, to fill the stretching silence.

"I have to go. I'm having the clambake for Ed and Sally."

It was the first time he'd referred to anything pleasant in their past, and as they got into Kurt's car, she continued the subject.

"How's their restaurant coming along?"

"Fine, it'll be opening in three weeks. They're back in the house already."

"That's good. Have you done much wind surfing?"

"No, I've been in New York all week."

Here a week, and he hadn't called her. She should be grateful—any call would have been in the nature of a tirade—but she felt cheated that she hadn't even known he was here. "Who's minding Brix?" she asked.

"Ed minds her when I have to be away."

This stilted exchange about exhausted their supply of small talk. The car cruised quietly through the streets. "Where do you live?"

"Upper East Side, Seventy-third." Another pall of silence fell. Shawna couldn't think of anything to say. She just wished he would drive faster, so she could flee inside her apartment and cry in peace. The car soon slid up to the door of her apartment house.

"Thanks for the lift. Don't bother getting out," Shawna said, opening her own door. So it was going to end this way, in a pointless, polite parting. She hesitated a moment. At least he'd say good-night.

Kurt looked at her uncertainly. He had no intention of forgiving Shawna Cassidy. She'd deceived him, made a fool of him, lied and then hadn't even picked up the phone to say she was sorry. But when he looked at her woebegone little face, he knew he wasn't going to let her walk away like this. "It's not late," he said. "Would you like to go somewhere for a nightcap?"

Shawna's first surge of pleasure soon dwindled to indecision. She studied him, trying to see if he was just being polite, or if he really wanted to continue this meeting. Annoyance seemed to be his predominant emotion. She didn't need any more ill humor.

"I guess not, thanks. You'll want an early start tomorrow."

"I'm not leaving until noon. I fly to Portland." He looked at her questioningly. His anger had turned to boredom. And the boredom must be just an act. Why did he persist?

"Would you like to come up to my place for a drink?" she asked.

"Sure, why not?" Shawna directed him to a public parking lot down the street. They walked back to her apartment and went up the elevator. The mood was still uneven, and Shawna had the awful feeling Kurt was only here to make amends for being rude at the party. This had been a terrible idea. She didn't have anything to drink but wine coolers and soda pop. Kurt probably hated wine coolers. Her apartment would look tiny and mediocre to him. Very likely he lived at Sutton Place.

"I only have a studio," she explained. "Rents are so high in New York."

"It's a nice building, anyway," he said.

The little apartment was tidy and decorated with style, if not much money. Framed prints lent a dash of color to the off-white walls, and the bed was made up into a sofa, piled with bright cushions. A drafting table and chair occupied one corner of the room.

"Would you like a wine cooler, or a wine cooler?" she asked with a shrug. "Or I have some cola..."

"Cola's fine."

"I'll be right back."

Shawna escaped to the kitchen and poured two soft drinks over ice. When she returned, Kurt was at the drafting board, examining her sketch. She had drawn a faceless head and body outline, concentrating on the dress.

Kurt seemed out of place in her cramped little home. Even in his jacket and dress jeans, he had an air of easy elegance, a presence that lent him distinction. He looked up and smiled the first real smile she'd seen since leaving Maine.

"No camera! I'm just looking." Kurt held up his hands defensively.

"Let's not rattle that skeleton, okay?" She handed him a glass and they stood together, studying her design of a sun dress.

"This isn't bad," Kurt said consideringly. "What material do you plan to use?"

"A light cotton, in some wild print. Big, bold polka dots, maybe black on yellow. What do you think?"

Kurt picked up the charcoal and began drawing the dots. Shawna watched as his hand moved with sure, strong strokes.

"Bigger," she said, and took the charcoal from him to show the size.

When she was finished, Kurt took a red oil pastel and sketched Shawna's hairstyle on the faceless model, with one long wave falling over her eye. A quick movement of the hand, and he had added a suggestion of her face. "You designed this one for you, right?"

"I usually design what I'd like to wear myself. I think I'm a fairly typical consumer, more interested in looking good and feeling comfortable than in wearing haute couture."

"Is what you're wearing your own design?" he asked, examining her critically. "It fills both criteria. Very chic."

She felt a small glow of pleasure. Praise from Slater really meant something. "This was one of my projects in college," she explained.

"Nice." His gaze skimmed over the short cut of the top, lingering a moment at the bare midriff, and moving down to the pleated trousers, without giving the impression that he was assessing her body. It was a businesslike examination. "You should do well with Irene."

"I'm going to give it my best shot."

They strolled to the sofa and sat down. The awful feeling of constraint was dissipating. Talking shop seemed to distract them from other tensions. For the next half hour, they discussed their work.

"I started out in college as a commercial artist," Kurt said, "but I always found myself more interested in drawing people than still lifes with apples and grapes, or whatever. Eventually my interest began to focus on fashion design. After a bit of soul-searching I switched to design. I've never looked back."

"I was never interested in anything but fashion design. My mom and everybody told me I should be a model, since I'm so tall and skinny, but I wanted to make the clothes. I used to try on my mother's gowns. She had some dynamite clothes, too."

"She would, being Everett's favorite model."

"Yes." Shawna gave him a leery look as this unwelcome topic reared its head again.

"We can't just push it under the rug, Shawna," Kurt said, pinning her with a long, searching, unfathomable look.

"I know. I guess I shouldn't have believed Everett. But he was like an uncle to me. I never even questioned it when he told me that story about you. I just assumed that because he said it, it must be true."

Kurt nodded. "Trust isn't such a bad quality. I probably would have done the same thing myself. I was mad as a hornet when Nancy told me you worked for Everett. It was the deception that bothered me more than the rest of it. I couldn't believe it. And when I went into the house and saw you with those sketches spread out, actually taking pictures of them..."

"I know," Shawna moaned.

"No, you don't," he said simply. "I was too upset to see what you were photographing at first. I thought you were taking pictures of my new line, to take back to Everett. I just wanted to—"

"Imagine how *I* felt when I saw Everett's sketches locked away in *your* closet," she pointed out. Memories of that awful incident clouded her eyes. "Why did you keep them?"

"I don't know. Nancy brought them to me a few days before Everett's show, to demonstrate the similarities to my work. I had intended to confront him, but Everett had altered the designs enough so that I couldn't prove anything. And at the time, I didn't know how he could have gotten copies of my sketches. Later I learned one of my employees had arranged it. After the dust settled, I just stuck Everett's designs away in the cabinet and forgot them. You really thought I was the thief?"

His brooding eyes examined her minutely. There was accusation and pain in that look. She would have given anything to be able to deny it. "I wouldn't have been there if I hadn't," she admitted.

Kurt's voice was taking on that hard edge again when he replied. "I guess we just chalk this one up to experience."

"I guess so. You live and learn."

"Yeah." The muscle at the back of Kurt's jaws moved in irritation. He set down his glass. "Thanks for the drink, Shawna. I'm glad we had this talk, to clear the air.''

She didn't want him to leave on this abrupt note. ''Before you go, what did you say to Everett? What did *he* say when you confronted him?''

''He told me I should be flattered, that he wouldn't steal from anyone but the best. I *was* flattered, too,'' he admitted. ''In his day, Everett *was* the best. I told him if he ever tried that stunt again, I'd knock his head off. He said plagiarizing would be difficult from Paris. He had decided to leave, and did I really think it in the best interest of the industry for me to publicize this contretemps. I said no, providing he remained in Paris.''

Shawna could picture that meeting vividly; Everett refusing to grovel, or even admit he'd done wrong. Kurt had been extremely generous, given that kind of provocation. ''It all sounds very civilized,'' she said.

''We tried to keep it that way. I couldn't help feeling a little sorry for him.''

''Did he mention me?''

''Your name didn't come up. We were being too civilized to get down to the nitty-gritty of just how he planned to snitch my designs this time.''

''I suggested he go and see you,'' Shawna said, looking hopefully for a word of approval.

''That's not why he came. I suggested it, too, rather peremptorily. And now let's forget this distasteful subject, once and for all. We'll probably be meeting from time to time in future, since we're both in the business. It'll be better if we don't meet as enemies.''

A lump grew in her throat. Her hopes had soared beyond not being enemies, but even for that she was grateful. "I'm sorry things worked out this way, Kurt."

"That's rather a lenient choice of phrase. Things didn't just 'work out this way,' Shawna. *You* worked them out. You came to Maine for the purpose of sabotaging me. Oh, I know you were misled by Everett, but wouldn't it have been only decent behavior on your part to have phoned me and apologized when you learned the truth?"

"I wanted to, Kurt. I was afraid of what you'd say. I told you, I'm sorry. I told Nancy to tell you."

"You should have told me yourself!" he snapped. "Some things should be handled in person. You don't send a message like that through a third party, a mere acquaintance. How do you think I felt when I learned the woman I loved and trusted was stabbing me in the back?"

"I know *exactly* how you felt!"

Kurt looked at her, frowning. "If that's true, if you had come to love me, too, then your not telling the truth is even worse. And your not explaining to me in person is incredible." He examined her, waiting to see if she had any explanation. Although she looked like a whipped puppy, she didn't say anything. "You don't have to pretend anything now, Shawna. It's all over. I didn't come here to lecture. This time we're really finished with the whole Everett affair." He rose. "Goodbye, Shawna."

Shawna couldn't trust her legs to try to stand up. She felt as if a steamroller had just run over her. "Goodbye, Kurt." It was a whisper of regret. Then he was gone, out of the apartment, out of her life.

Chapter Ten

After Kurt left, Shawna sat alone, thinking over the meeting. What astonished her most was that it hadn't occurred to her to phone him and explain the situation fully. She was racked with remorse. It was only common politeness—she had even urged Everett to do it, and felt quite sure Kurt would forgive him. So why hadn't she thought to phone Kurt herself? She'd been so preoccupied with the pain of losing him, with her fears of retribution, and with scurrying around to find a job, that she'd left the most important thing undone.

Even without calling him to apologize, he had forgiven her. Kurt was more than polite, more than kind. He was generous, but even his generosity had its limits, and he'd made it perfectly clear that in future they'd meet as nonenemies. He hadn't used the word friend. He had used the words, "the woman I loved," though. He had actually loved her. They might be together now, if only she hadn't botched the affair so badly. She could be attending the clambake for Ed and Sally with him tomorrow.

Monday morning at work, she found her mind reverting to that happy week at Spindrift Cottage, and thinking of the people she'd met there. After dinner that evening, she decided to phone Sally and wish her and Ed luck on their restaurant reopening. Sally answered the phone.

"I just wanted to wish you and Ed luck," Shawna said.

"Thanks, Shawna. I'm sorry you couldn't come for the clambake. It was terrific. The boys and I were really looking forward to having you for the weekend. They picked fresh flowers for your room and everything. Kurt explained that you were particularly busy now with your new job, but I hope you can come and see us later."

"Yes," Shawna replied, and managed to say a few words, while her mind reeled. Sally's conversation made it perfectly clear that she had asked Kurt to invite Shawna to visit her for the weekend. And he hadn't done it; he hadn't even mentioned it. It was a mere fluke that she'd phoned Sally and found out. She was furious with Kurt, then desolate. He didn't want her at his clambake. That's why he hadn't delivered Sally's message. If she'd been visiting the Browns, naturally she would have attended Kurt's party with them.

Over the next week Shawna learned that love didn't die just because you were angry with the love object, and just because you didn't see him. The anger subsided, but the sorrow remained. Her life was busy with all the commotion of settling into her new job, meeting new people and finally learning from someone who appreciated her designs. Her new life was exciting and fun, but like sunshine on a stormy sea, it only concealed the turmoil below. It didn't tame it. Nothing would heal her heart unless she settled this relationship once and for all. She had to find out if there was a chance for her and Kurt. If the answer was no, then maybe the convalescence could begin.

As Kurt didn't call her, Shawna realized it was going to be up to her to make the first move. She thought and thought about it, and finally chose a meeting that might tempt him. She'd have a clambake of her own. She would invite her old friends from Everetts and her new friends from Renfrews to Connecticut for an old-fashioned clambake. And she'd invite Kurt, too.

If he refused without giving her a solid reason, she would assume her case was hopeless. Or if he accepted from mere politeness to a colleague, the other guests would make it possible for him to be friendly without committing himself. But if he still felt something for her, he'd find an opportunity to tell her. In this way, she was making the overture, but she could keep her self-respect if Kurt wasn't interested.

Shawna phoned her mother to arrange the party for the next Saturday. Adele had already made plans to visit her sister in Chicago that weekend, but she offered to do the preliminary ordering of food and drinks. Shawna invited her friends in New York and was pleased that most of them could come. When it was time to call Kurt, she was plagued by an overwhelming reluctance to pick up the phone. If he said no, she didn't see how she could go on living.

She phoned him at his apartment on Sunday afternoon, but there was no answer. He didn't answer the phone at his cottage in Maine, either. On Monday morning she phoned his office from work, and was told he'd be in on Tuesday. On Tuesday she called again, and Nancy Alton answered. Nancy had already accepted an invitation to the clambake.

"Kurt had to fly out to the West Coast for the week, Shawna. Can I help, or is this personal?"

"I wanted to ask him to my party Saturday." But calling all the way to California to do it seemed pushy.

"I don't know where he's staying in L.A. He has friends, but sometimes he stays at a hotel. He'll be calling the office, and I can pass along the invitation. Will that do?"

"That'll be fine," Shawna agreed, feeling a cowardly wave of relief that she didn't have to ask him herself.

"I'm not sure he'll be back in time. He's out scrounging up materials for the line. They have such interesting small textile plants on the West Coast. But I'll be at your party anyway. I'm looking forward to it."

Shawna gave Nancy directions to her mother's house and hung up, still in turmoil. He might not even be back in time. She should have asked Kurt first, and arranged the party for a time he could attend. But she did want to entertain her friends, and she knew they'd have a good time with or without Kurt Slater.

Irene let her off early Friday to go home and take care of the necessary preparations. As Shawna approached the coast, the scent of the sea came wafting toward her, carrying on its mist a host of memories.

Her mother had hired a local couple, the Kesslers, to help with the cooking and serving. The lobsters and corn and clams would be delivered early Saturday afternoon. The drinks were already there, and Shawna would handle the last-minute details. As she drove her mother to the airport Friday night, they talked about Everett.

"Have you heard from Uncle Max since he left for Paris?" Shawna asked.

"He called me a few days ago. He loves Paris. I don't know why he waited so long to go. It's his natural home. He's found a shop to hire just off the Champs Elysées, and is having a ball decorating it."

"I kind of thought when Dad died that you and Everett might get together."

"Me and Everett!" her mother howled. "Where on earth did you get that idea?"

"He seemed crazy about you, and I thought you liked him."

"Oh, no, Shawna. First I worked for him, and admired his creations. Later we just met socially from time to time. I'd call him when I went to New York. Everett liked to be seen with me. We always caused a stir when we went out—people haven't quite forgotten me, and Everett liked the attention."

"But he often visited you in Connecticut."

"Everett's a great visitor. I suppose he misses not having a family of his own. He never married. Fashion was his wife, he used to say. He'd bring me all the gossip about old friends, that's all. There was no passion."

"I see."

"I'm very angry with him at the moment. He might have told you before you went to work for him that he was leaving the States," Adele continued. "It was a waste of your time, but that's Everett all over. He only thinks of himself. At least you've landed a new job. How do you like working for Renfrews?"

They talked about Shawna's new job till they reached the airport, then Shawna went home alone. She had invited a few local friends to the clambake, and one of them, Shirley Horton, came over that evening for a visit. She helped Shawna set out the dishes and haul the big kettle out of storage.

On Saturday morning they strung Japanese lanterns around the patio. Adele had tended her garden before she left, and the effect was beautiful. The Kesslers arrived to start the cooking and set up the bar. The day passed in a confused whirl of activity, but if Shawna was out of the house for as much as five minutes, the first thing she did when she came in was check the telephone answering machine.

There was no word from Kurt. She didn't know if he'd be coming, or if he'd even gotten her message. For all she knew, he was still in L.A. Her guests were invited for seven, to have drinks on the patio and help with the cooking. At six, Shirley said, "I better go home now and get dressed. With all your fashion-conscious friends here, I'll have to make a special effort. Are any big names coming?"

"Irene Renfrew will be here," Shawna reminded her.

"She's terrific, but I mean the real biggies. Anybody like Slater?"

"I invited him," Shawna said nonchalantly. "He may not be able to make it. He's on the West Coast."

Shirley stared in amazement. "You mean you actually know him? I was only kidding. Oh, Shawna, I hope he comes. He's a doll."

"I met him in Maine," Shawna said briefly. She hadn't told Shirley anything about that interlude. She could hardly say the name Slater without trembling.

Shirley left, and Shawna went upstairs to shower and dress. A clambake was definitely casual, but it was a special occasion, and she wore a long, swirling emerald-green skirt, with a crisp white shoulderless top. Fishing through her mother's dresser, she found a black belt with a dazzling rhinestone clasp—subtle but elegant.

Although the evening was sultry, the weather forecast was for clear weather, so that was one problem avoided. As Shawna brushed her hair and put on makeup, she noticed the febrile glitter in her eyes. Two spots of red stood out on her cheeks, and she felt nearly ill from worry.

Kurt couldn't be coming. He would have notified her. He would have phoned for directions to her house. When the phone rang, she jumped a foot and raced to answer it. It was Shirley Horton. "I forgot to ask you, will there be swimming?"

"If you want to. It's pretty warm, but I doubt if the others will get in the water."

"I'll bring my suit just in case."

"Okay, see you soon."

At ten to seven Shawna went out to the patio, and enjoyed the cooling breeze from the ocean. The Kesslers were busy preparing the clam kettle with seaweed and fixing the fire. Shawna checked to see that everything looked its best. Her mother was an avid gardener, and this patio was her living room in the summer.

Barrels of flowers stood along the edge of the long concrete deck. Bright geraniums stood up in the center, edged with trailing ivies, vinca and purple lobelia, as dainty as lace. A terraced English garden along one side was a riot of color. Golden crown and huge white daisies vied with zinnias and petunias, planted annually to give a rich effect. Behind them, the delphiniums stood proudly erect, with sweet peas climbing against the cedar fence. Every square inch of land was blooming.

The house was quite different from the more traditional architecture of Maine. Adele's house was a rambling, modern bungalow, built of salmon-colored brick. A picture window gave her a view of her garden from the living room when the weather made it impossible for her to be out there.

Shawna found herself wondering what Kurt would think of it. It was more ornate than his plain Cape Cod cottage, but it gave the same feeling of warmth and hospitality. He'd like it, she decided—if he came, that is.

Shirley was the only one to arrive promptly at seven. By seven-fifteen the first guests from New York arrived, and by seven-thirty most of the group had assembled.

Their reactions were always the same. "What a lovely place, Shawna! And that ocean breeze—divine! How can you bear to leave it in summer?" Then a quick trip to the bar. "I'm parched. That drive was hot."

By eight, Shawna assumed everyone who was coming had arrived—and Kurt wasn't here. She approached Nancy Alton.

"Did you have any trouble finding the place?"

"Not at all, your directions were good. Who's the gardener?"

"I can't take any credit. This is Mom's hobby, or should I say avocation."

After they had admired the large, colorful blossoms, Shawna mustered her courage and asked, "Did you hear from Kurt? I guess he couldn't make it, huh?"

"He was held up at the airport in L.A. last night. There was a storm on the West Coast, you know."

"I hadn't heard. I was so worried about the weather on the East Coast that I hadn't thought of that."

"He said he'd try to make it," Nancy added. "This was a lovely idea," she continued. "It's nice to mingle with people from the other fashion houses."

He'd try to make it—that was some small consolation. Or was it just politeness?

As the kettle boiled, the smell of cooking seafood began wafting over the patio, reminding the guests how hungry they were. Soon the top layer of clams was ready, and the crowd lined up with their plates to start the feast. They ate outdoors in groups, some at picnic tables and some balancing plates in their laps.

Shawna was busy playing the hostess, passing salads and rolls and filling glasses. She was glad to keep busy. It distracted her from the growing swell of sadness inside. He wasn't coming. Kurt wasn't coming. When the layers had all been eaten through, the clams and green corn and finally the lobster, the guests were tempted by a trolley of French pastries.

Shawna served them, smiling at the lively and colorful scene. She loved parties like this, where everyone was relaxed and having a good time. Her boss, Irene, complimented her a dozen times. When everyone had eaten to repletion, the Kesslers cleared the patio and Shawna played tapes for dancing, with the loudspeakers strung out to the patio.

The last streaks of red sunk below the horizon, and the Japanese lanterns now illuminated the velvety night as they bounced jauntily in the breeze. A colleague, Mike Gainer, asked Shawna to dance, and she accepted. She danced twice with Mike, then with some other men, smiling till her face ached with the strain. Would it never be over? It was a quarter after eleven, and her guests still had to drive back to Manhattan.

"We really should be going," Irene said with a reluctant sigh.

"Why don't I make some coffee?" Shawna suggested.

"That's a good idea."

Shawna went into the kitchen and watched the coffee perk. Mrs. Kessler took a tray of cups and cream and sugar out to the patio. But Shawna didn't feel up to joining her own party, a gathering that had about as much pleasure for her as a wake. When the coffee was ready, she carried the pot out to the patio, walking carefully to avoid spilling it, or burning herself.

When she got to the door, she saw Kurt Slater coming down the path behind the terraced garden. She thought she was hallucinating. There was a strange ringing in her ears, and the heavy coffee urn trembled in her hands. It couldn't be! He wouldn't come at eleven-thirty, when everyone else was talking about leaving. He hadn't driven all the way from New York after flying in from L.A. just to stay half an hour. Unless...

She went out and put the urn on the table, where Mrs. Kessler waited with the cups. A few people had already lined up. From the corner of her eye she saw Kurt standing at the top of the steps, scanning the crowd—for her—surely for her. He was shielded by bushes, and no one else had seen him yet. As the hostess, it was her job to welcome him, and she took a deep breath to steady her nerves for the encounter.

Kurt spotted her, and began hurrying toward her. They met just at the bottom of the staircase. An awful feeling of constraint hovered over them.

"I'm glad you could come, Kurt," she said, hating the cool sound of her voice.

"I was afraid I'd missed it. Better late than never." Kurt's gaze flickered around the flowers, then out to the water beyond. "This is a lovely place."

"Thank you. I'd offer you some food, but I'm afraid you've missed the best part. Would you like some dessert and coffee?"

"I didn't really come for food," he said, looking at her with a tentative question in his eyes.

Before Shawna could reply, Nancy spotted Kurt and came forward to welcome him. "Kurt!" Other heads turned, and a ripple of excitement ran through the party as the news spread. It seemed everyone was staring in his direction. Shawna saw Shirley Horton watching wide-eyed. Kurt was treated as a celebrity by his colleagues, and while Shawna was proud for him, it ruined their privacy.

With hostess duties to perform, Shawna glided quietly away to help Mrs. Kessler at the coffee table. Over the next half hour, Shawna found her gaze turning often to Kurt. His sport shirt was blue and white striped, and although he wore jeans with it he still stood out in the crowd.

His proud head was a few inches higher than most, giving a clear view of his distinct features. Her original impression of him was restored. He looked savage, with those high cheekbones, a square chin and a dark tan. His strongly arched, mobile eyebrows framed his devastating eyes. Glancing at her female guests, Shawna realized she wasn't the only one who was mesmerized by him. Their reaction stopped just short of fawning.

The guests who had planned to have a quick coffee and leave settled down for another half hour. That half hour seemed longer than the rest of the day and evening together. It seemed no one wanted to go while

Kurt stayed, and that meant no opportunities for Shawna.

The coffeepot was empty, and it was after midnight before the subject of leaving came up again. Finally, the tired guests began to murmur their final thanks and prepare to leave. Shawna stood and thanked them for coming. She was afraid Kurt would line up with the others and leave, too, but when she looked around, there was no sign of him. Had he left already, without even saying goodbye? She had to keep smiling till she could be alone. It wasn't till the last guest, Shirley Horton, waved goodbye and scampered home through the hedge that Kurt reappeared.

He peeked out through the kitchen door. "Are they all gone yet?" he asked. The way he said it sounded as if he'd also been waiting for everyone else to leave.

"Oh, you're still here, Kurt!" she exclaimed in surprise.

Kurt gave her a peculiar, questioning look. "I arrived late," he reminded her. "Doesn't that entitle me to five minutes alone with my hostess?"

"Of course. I wasn't hinting that you should leave!" she said hurriedly. "I just didn't see you, and thought . . ."

"I was hiding," he admitted.

"You were escaping from your fans!"

"You make me sound pretty conceited."

"No, just inventive," she complimented. "They were preparing to leave before you arrived."

Kurt took her hand and they walked out beyond the patio, down to the water's edge, as if by tacit agreement. Away from the house lights, the moon's paler illumination lent a romantic aura to the view. They didn't speak till they came to the water.

Kurt was gazing out at the moon-dappled waves, and Shawna peered up at him, trying to read his mood. "I'm glad you could come," she said. "Nancy told me there was a storm on the West Coast."

"I was afraid I wasn't going to make it." He turned his head and gazed down at her. "I should have replied to your invitation, but I didn't know whether I'd be able to come or not. I didn't like to refuse, but I didn't want to say yes, and then not show up, either."

"That's all right. It doesn't matter, Kurt. But you missed a great clambake," she added.

The wind ruffled her hair, blowing the long wave in her eyes. Unthinkingly Kurt reached out and pushed it back, then stood, looking at her intently. The intimate gesture warmed her, till she noticed his expression.

"So you were familiar with clambakes," he said accusingly. Shawna had treated him like a stooge. She had pretended to be someone she wasn't. The sophisticated life was nothing new to her. She had accused him of stealing, and betrayed his trust and friendship by using his own key to search his house. When the affair was over, she hadn't even told him why she'd done it. And yet, he was ready to forgive it all. He was so eager to forgive that he'd risked his neck to get here, only to hear her say "It doesn't matter."

What was hardest to forgive was that she'd used his love to perpetrate her scheme. Had she just pretended to love him? When he looked at her face in the moonlight, it was hard to believe it had all been an act. She looked uncertain and wistful, but her eyes gleamed with some other emotion.

"Why did you invite me here, Shawna?" he asked quietly.

She met his gaze steadily. Her nerves felt taut, drawn tight and tense as piano wire. "Because I wanted to see you."

"You didn't have to entertain half of New York to accomplish that. All you had to do was lift the phone," he pointed out reasonably.

"It's not that easy. I called you several times, but couldn't reach you."

"What I'm trying to discover is whether the invitation was just a gesture of goodwill to a colleague, or—" His dark brow rose in a question.

Shawna considered her answer. "I wanted to tell you I'm sorry about Maine. Not just about spying, but all of it—letting on I was a secretary. It was a necessary part of the deception. Other than changing jobs, the rest of me was real, Kurt. I did enjoy our time together. It would have been perfect if it could have happened without any intrigue...." Her words trailed off.

"About why I invited you here, I wanted you to have a chance to refuse politely if you didn't want to see me. It was kind of a—test, I suppose," she admitted.

Kurt smiled ruefully. "I guess that's what I wanted to hear. I wanted to know it wasn't all an act. That you really do enjoy the simple life, that we have that important element in common."

She gave him an impish smile. "Sure I enjoy it. I would have enjoyed visiting the Browns for a weekend, too—if I'd received their invitation."

A wave of guilt flickered in Kurt's eyes. "You've been talking to Sally. I guess you're not the only one with a bit of apologizing to do. I was within a heartbeat of asking you to come with me that weekend."

"Why didn't you?"

Kurt shook his head, frowning. "I don't know. Self-defense, maybe. I needed a bit of time to think things out, and I knew if you were there, my heart would overrule my head."

Shawna looked at him expectantly. "But you came to my party tonight..."

"I didn't drive to Palm Springs in the middle of a deluge and hire a chartered plane to New York just to attend another fashion party. The airport at L.A. was closed down."

"Kurt! You did all that!" His lingering gaze confirmed her first quick hope. It was the look he'd worn in Maine, when they were first falling in love. A look composed of gentleness, surprise and passion.

"All that, and I wasn't even sure I'd be here before the party was over," he said, drawing her into his arms.

A smile shone on her elfin face as she looped her arms around his neck. "I think the real party's just beginning," she whispered in a breathless voice.

"Let's be up front with each other this time, okay?" Kurt said. "No secrets. No tricks. I love you, Shawna. Will you marry me?"

A swell of joy grew in her. Her arms tightened around his neck, pulling him closer as she told him all the things she'd been wanting to say for so long. "Yes! Oh, and I love you, too, Kurt."

A flame leaped in his eyes, and his arms crushed her against him.

"I hated deceiving you in Maine, but I couldn't let that stop me from doing what I had to do—what I thought I had to do, I mean," she said, the words tumbling out confusedly. "I should have explained. I don't know why I didn't think of it. It's only common courtesy, and to add that to the rest of it. I wouldn't blame you if you never spoke to me again."

"Slow down." He laughed. "Give a guy a chance to get a kiss in edgewise, will you?"

The first tender brushing of their lips caused a swelling of love, which expanded till her whole body quivered with it. The embrace intensified, enfolding them in its magic.

She felt his lips slide across her cheek, leaving a trail of kisses till they reached her ear. "I was never so miserable in my life as I've been the last weeks," he said in a voice husky with love. "It was so perfect, wasn't it, sweetheart? I felt I'd found my other half. It was like losing a part of myself when you left. We'll recapture that magic. It'll be even better. I'll have you in New York, too—as my wife."

"And I'll have you in Maine." She sighed happily.

"On the weekends, I'll teach you to wind surf."

"I *know* how to wind surf!"

"Mmm." His lips found her earlobe and seized it. "Then I'll have to teach you something else. Any ideas?" he asked, in a voice of silken suggestion.

A tingle of fire seared along her veins, making her breaths uneven. "I guess you could teach me a little something about designing."

"That wasn't what I had in mind. I was thinking of—this." His lips found hers again and attacked them.

The moon shone on the dark ocean, but behind Shawna's closed eyes it felt like the heat of the sun, warm, life-giving, and everlasting.

*   *   *   *   *

Silhouette Romance

LONG, TALL TEXANS

A Trilogy by Diana Palmer

Bestselling Diana Palmer has rustled up three rugged heroes in a trilogy sure to lasso your heart! The titles of the books are your introduction to these unforgettable men:

CALHOUN

In June, meet Calhoun Ballenger. He wants to protect Abby Clark from the world, but can he protect her from himself?

JUSTIN

Calhoun's brother, Justin—the strong, silent type—has a second chance with the woman of his dreams, Shelby Jacobs, in August.

TYLER

October's long, tall Texan is Shelby's virile brother, Tyler, who teaches shy Nell Regan to trust her instincts—especially when they lead her into his arms!

Don't miss CALHOUN, JUSTIN and TYLER—three gripping new stories coming soon from Silhouette Romance!

SRLTT

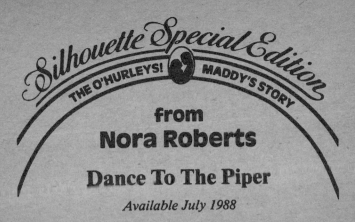

Silhouette Special Edition

THE O'HURLEYS! MADDY'S STORY

from
Nora Roberts

Dance To The Piper

Available July 1988

The second in an exciting new series about the lives and
loves of triplet sisters—

If *The Last Honest Woman* (SE #451) captured your
heart in May, you're sure to want to read about Maddy
and Chantel, Abby's two sisters.

In *Dance to the Piper* (SE #463), it takes some very
fancy footwork to get reserved recording mogul Reed
Valentine dancing to effervescent Maddy's tune....

Then, in *Skin Deep* (SE #475), find out what kind of
heat it takes to melt the glamorous Chantel's icy heart.
Available in September.

THE O'HURLEYS!

**Join the excitement of
Silhouette Special Editions.**

COMING NEXT MONTH

#592 JUSTIN—Diana Palmer
Book 2 in the LONG, TALL TEXANS Trilogy!
Rugged cowboy Justin Ballenger was the man of Shelby Jacobs's dreams, but years ago circumstances had ended their engagement, leaving Justin brokenhearted and bitter. Could Shelby convince him she'd never stopped loving him?

#593 SHERLOCK'S HOME—Sharon De Vita
Arrogant detective Mike Ryce wanted to be little T. C. Sherlock's foster father, but welfare agent Wilhelmina Walker thought he was wrong for the job. So why was Mike gaining custody of her heart?

#594 FINISHING TOUCH—Jane Bierce
Clay Dowling's corporation was threatening to destroy Rose Davis's cozy cottage. She had to fight him, but would she lose her heart to his Southern charm before she won the war?

#595 THE LADYBUG LADY—Pamela Toth
From the moment Cassie Culpepper sprayed Jack Hoffman with the garden hose to keep him from killing her ladybugs, she'd captured his attention. Now he wanted the lovely Ladybug Lady to fly—straight to *his* home....

#596 A NIGHT OF PASSION—Lucy Gordon
The greatest joy in Veronica Grant's life had begun with one night of passion in Jordan Cavendish's arms. But she'd kept their child a secret, and now she and her daughter desperately needed Jordan's help....

#597 THE KISS OF A STRANGER—Brittany Young
In the Scottish Highlands, Clarissa Michaels met James Maxwell, the man who had claimed her heart with one kiss. But Clarissa's life was in danger while she stayed in James's ancestral castle. Had destiny brought them together only to tear them apart?

AVAILABLE THIS MONTH:

Silhouette Intimate Moments

At Dodd Memorial Hospital, Love is the Best Medicine

When temperatures are rising and pulses are racing, Dodd Memorial Hospital is the place to be. Every doctor, nurse and patient is a heart specialist, and their favorite prescription is a little romance. This month, finish Lucy Hamilton's Dodd Memorial Hospital Trilogy with HEARTBEATS, IM #245.

Nurse Vanessa Rice thought police sergeant Clay Williams was the most annoying man she knew. Then he showed up at Dodd Memorial with a gunshot wound, and the least she could do was be friends with him—if he'd let her. But Clay was interested in something more, and Vanessa didn't want that kind of commitment. She had a career that was important to her, and there was no room in her life for any man. But Clay was determined to show her that they could have a future together—and that there are times when the patient knows best.
